NAN SHERWOOD AT ROSE RANCH

OR

THE OLD MEXICAN'S TREASURE

BY

ANNIE ROE CARR

Nan Sherwood at Rose Ranch; Or, The Old Mexican's Treasure

Annie Roe Carr

CONTENTS

I. SCHOOL REOPENS

II. INTRODUCTIONS

III. "CURFEW SHALL NOT RING TO-NIGHT"

IV. WALKING THE PLANK

V. RHODA IS UNPOPULAR

VI. THE MEXICAN GIRL

VII. DOWN THE SLOPE

VIII. AFTERNOON TEA

IX. NOT ALWAYS "BUTTERFINGERS"

X. THE TREASURE OF ROSE RANCH

XI. JUANITA

XII. ROSE RANCH AT LAST

XIII. OPEN SPACES

XIV. THE POOR LITTLE CALF

XV. A TROPHY FOR ROOM EIGHT

XVI. EXPECTATIONS

XVII. THE ROUND-UP

XVIII. THE OUTLAW

XIX. A RAID

XX. THE ANTELOPE HUNT; AND MORE

XXI. IN THE OLD BEAR DEN

XXII. AFTER THE TEMPEST

XXIII. THE LETTER FROM JUANITA

XXIV. UNCERTAINTIES

XXV. THE STAMPEDE

XXVI. WHO ARE THEY?

XXVII. THE FUNNEL

XXVIII. A PRISONER

XXIX. A TAMED OUTLAW

XXX. TREASURE-TROVE

CHAPTER I

SCHOOL REOPENS

"And of course," drawled Laura Polk, she of the irrepressible spirits and what Mrs. Cupp called "flamboyant" hair, "she will come riding up to the Hall on her trusty pinto pony (whatever kind of pony that is), with a gun at her belt and swinging a lariat. She will yell for Dr. Beulah to come forth, and the minute the darling appears this Rude Rhoda from the Rolling Prairie will proceed to rope our dear preceptress and bear her off captive to her lair—"

"My—goodness—gracious—Agnes!" exclaimed Amelia Boggs, more frequently addressed as 'Procrastination Boggs', "you are getting your metaphors dreadfully mixed. It is a four-legged beast of prey that bears its victim away to its 'lair.'"

"How do you know Rollicking Rhoda from Crimson Gulch hasn't four legs?" demanded the red-haired girl earnestly. "You know very well from what we see in the movies that there are more wonders in the 'Wild and Woolly West' than are dreamed of in your philosophy, Horatio-Amelia."

"One thing I say," said a very much overdressed girl who had evidently just arrived, for she had not removed her furs and coat, and was warming herself before the open fire in the beautiful reception hall where this conversation was going on, "I think Lakeview Hall is getting to be dreadfully common, when all sorts and conditions of girls are allowed to come here."

"Oh, I guess this Rhododendron-girl from Dead Man's Den has money enough to suit even you, Linda," Laura Polk said carelessly.

"Money isn't everything, I hope," said the girl in furs, tossing her head.

"Hear! Hear!" exclaimed Laura, and some of the other girls laughed. "Linda's had a change of heart."

"Dear me!" sniffed Linda Riggs, "how smart you are, Polk. Just as though I was not used to anything but money—"

"True. You are. But you have never talked about much of anything else before this particular occasion," said the red-haired girl. "What has happened to you, Linda mine, since you separated from us all at the beginning of the winter holidays?"

Linda merely sniffed again and turned to speak to her particular chum, Cora Courtney.

"You should have been with me in Chicago, Cora—at my cousin, Pearl Graves', house. I tried to get Pearl—she's just about our age—to come to Lakeview Hall; but she goes to a private school right in her neighborhood—oh! a *very* select place. No girl like this wild Western person Polk is talking about, would be received there. No, indeed!"

"Hi, Linda!" broke in the irrepressible red-haired girl, "why didn't you try to enter that wonderful school?"

"I did ask to. But my father is *so* old-fashioned," complained Linda. "He would not hear of it. Said it would not be treating Dr. Beulah right."

"Oh, oh!" groaned Laura. "How the dear doctor would have suffered, Linda, if you had not come back to her sheltering arms."

The laugh this raised among the party made Linda's cheeks flame more hotly than before. She would not look at the laughing group again. A flaxen-haired girl with pink cheeks and blue eyes—one of the smallest though not the youngest in the party—came timidly to Linda Riggs' elbow.

"Did you spend all your vacation in Chicago?" she asked gently. "I was to go to visit Grace; but there was sickness at home, and so I couldn't. Didn't the Masons come back with you, Linda?"

"And Nan Sherwood and Bess Harley?" questioned Amelia Boggs, the homely girl. "They went to the Masons' to visit, didn't they?"

"I'm sure I could not tell you much about *them*," Linda said, shrugging her shoulders. "I had something else to do, I can assure you, than to look up Sherwood and Harley."

"Why!" gasped the fair-haired girl, "Grace wrote me that you were at her house, and went to the theater with them, and that—that—"

"Well, what of it, Lillie Nevins?" demanded the other sharply.

"In her letter she said you had a dreadful accident. That you were run away with in a sleigh and that Nan Sherwood and Walter saved your life."

"That sounds interesting!" cried Laura Polk. "So Our Nan has been playing the he-ro-wine again? How did it happen?"

"She has been putting herself forward the same as usual," snapped Linda Riggs. "I suppose that is what you mean. And Grace is crazy. Walter did help me when Madam Graves' horses ran away; but Nan Sherwood had nothing to do with it. Or, nothing much, at least."

"Keep on," said Laura Polk, dryly, "and I guess we'll get the facts of the case."

"If you think I am going to join this crew that praises Nan Sherwood to the skies, you are mistaken," cried Linda.

"All right. We'll hear all about it when Bess Harley comes," said Laura, laughing. She did like to plague Linda Riggs.

"Where are Nan and Bess, to say nothing of Gracie?" Amelia Boggs wanted to know. "You came on the last train, didn't you, Linda?"

"Oh, I did not pay much attention to those on the train," said Linda airily. "Father had his private car put on for me, and I rode in that."

Mr. Riggs was president of the railroad, and by no chance did his daughter ever let her mates lose sight of that fact.

"My goodness!" exclaimed Cora, "didn't you have anybody with you?"

"Well, no. You see, I invited Walter and Grace Mason, but they had people in the chair car they thought they must entertain," and she sniffed again.

"Oh, you Linda!" laughed Laura. "I bet I know who they were entertaining."

"Here comes the bus!" cried Amelia suddenly.

A rush of more than half the girls gathered about the open hearth for the great main entrance door of Lakeview Hall followed the announcement. This hall was almost like a castle set upon a high cliff overlooking Lake Huron on one side and the straggling town of Freeling, and Freeling Inlet, on the other.

The girls flung open the door. The school bus had just stopped before the wide veranda. Girls were fairly "boiling out of it," as Laura declared. Short, tall, thin, stout girls and girls of all ages between ten and seventeen tramped merrily up the steps with their handbags. Such a hullabaloo of greeting as there was!

"Come on, Cora," said Linda, haughtily. "Let us go up to our room. They are positively vulgar."

"Oh, no, Linda!" Cora cried. "I want to stay and see the fun."

"Fun!" gasped the disdainful Linda.

"Yes," said Cora, who was a terrible toady, but who showed some spirit on this occasion. "I want to have fun with the other girls. I don't want to be left out of everything just because of you. Even if you are going to flock by yourself this term, as you did most of last, because you are all the time quarreling with the girls that have the nicest times, I'm going to get into the fun."

This, according to Linda Riggs' opinion, was crass ingratitude and treachery. Besides, she and Cora had the nicest room in the Hall, for it had been fixed up especially for his daughter by Mr. Riggs; and Cora, who was poor, was allowed to be Linda's roommate without extra charge.

"You mean that you want to run with that Nan Sherwood and Bess Harley crew!" exclaimed Linda.

"I want to get into some of the fun. And so do you, Linda! Don't act offish," and Cora walked toward the open door to meet the new arrivals.

It was a terrible shock to the railroad magnate's daughter—this. The defection of her chief henchman and ally would rather break up the little group which Laura Polk had unkindly dubbed "the School of Snobs." With all her wealth Linda had but few retainers.

In the van of the newcomers were a rather comely, brown-eyed girl with a bright and cheerful expression of countenance, a dark beauty with curls and flashing eyes, and a demure but pretty girl to whom Lillie Nevins ran with exclamations of joy. This last was Grace Mason, the flaxen-haired girl's chum.

"Oh, Nancy! how well you look," cried Laura, hugging the brown-eyed girl. And to the curly-haired one: "What mischief have you got into, Bess? You look just as though you had done something."

"Don't say a word!" gasped Bess Harley in the red-haired girl's ear. "It's what we are going to do. Some sawneys have arrived. We'll have a procession."

"Oh, say!" exclaimed Amelia Boggs, "there is one special sawney expected. Did she come on this train with you other girls?"

"Oh, that's so! Who has seen Roistering Rhoda of the Staked Plains? Mrs. Cupp said she was due tonight," cried Laura.

"For goodness' sake!" exclaimed Bess, "who is that?"

"A sawney!" cried one of the other girls.

"They say she is Rhoda Hammond, from the very farthest West there is," Laura said gravely. "Of course she will ride in on a mustang, or something like that."

"What! with the snow two feet deep?" laughed the brown-eyed girl, tossing off her furs and smiling at the group of her schoolmates with happy mien.

"Say not so!" begged Laura. "No pony? What is the use of having a cow-girl fresh from the wildest West come to Lakeview Hall unless she comes in proper character?"

Nan Sherwood, having swept her old friends with her quick glance, now looked back at the group that had followed her into the hall. The bus had been so crowded and so dark that she had not known half of those who had been with her coming up from the Freeling railroad station.

"How nice it is to get back, isn't it?" she murmured to her special chum, Bess Harley.

"I should say!" agreed Elizabeth, warmly and emphatically.

Laura Polk, as an older girl and, after all, one of the most thoughtful, suddenly noticed a stranger in brown who still stood just inside the door that somebody had thoughtfully closed.

She made quite a charming, not to say striking, figure, as she stood there alone, just the faintest smile upon her lips, yet looking quite as neglected and lonely as any novice could possibly look.

This stranger wore brown furs and a brown coat, with a hat to match on which was a really wonderful brown plume. She wore bronze shoes and hose. Even Linda Riggs was dressed no more richly than this girl; only the latter was dressed in better taste than Linda.

Laura, leaving the gay company, went quickly toward the girl in brown and held out her hand.

"I am sure you are a stranger here," she said. "And I am a member of the Welcoming Committee. I am Laura Polk. And you—?"

"I am Rhoda Hammond," said the demure girl quietly.

"What!" almost shouted the startled Laura. "You're never! You can't be! Not Rollicking Rhoda from Rustlers' Roost, the wild Western adventuress we've heard so much about?"

"No," said the girl in brown, still placidly. "I am Rhoda Hammond from Rose Ranch."

CHAPTER II

INTRODUCTIONS

"Oh, my auntie!" murmured Amelia Boggs, using most uncommendable slang. "Stung!"

But Laura Polk, if inclined to be boisterous and rather rude in her jokes, was by no means petty. She burst into such a good-natured and disarming laugh that the girl in brown was forced to join her.

"There, Laura," said Bess Harley, "the biter for once is the bitten. I hope you are properly overcome."

Nan Sherwood likewise hastened to offer the new girl her hand.

"I am glad to greet you, Rhoda Hammond," she said sympathetically. "You must not mind our animal spirits. We just do slop over at this time, my dear. Wait till you see how gentle and decorous we have to be after the semester really begins. This is only letting off steam, you know."

"Do you meet all newcomers with the same grade of hospitality?" asked Rhoda Hammond, with more than a little sarcasm in both her words and tone.

"Only more so," Bess Harley assured her. "Oh, Nan! consider what they did to us when we came here for the first time last September. 'Member?"

Nan nodded with sudden gravity in her pretty face. She was not likely to forget that trying time. She had been on a very different footing with her schoolmates for the first few weeks of her life at Lakeview Hall than she was now.

Rhoda Hammond, the new girl, seemed to apprehend something of this change, for she said quickly and with much good sense:

"Well, if you two could stand it, and are evidently so much thought of now, I'll grin and bear it, too. Though it isn't just as we are taught to treat strangers out home. At Rose Ranch if a person is a tenderfoot we try to make it particularly easy for him."

"Oh, my dear," drawled Bess, her eyes dancing, "it works just the opposite at a girls' boarding school, believe me!"

Her chum, Nan, was for the moment not in a laughing mood. She could scarcely realize now that she was the same Nan Sherwood who had come so wonderingly and timidly to Lakeview Hall.

Of the Sherwoods there were only Nan and her father and mother. They were an especially warmly attached trio and probably, if a most wonderful and startling thing had not happened, Nan and Momsey and Papa Sherwood would never have been separated, or been fairly shaken out of their family existence, as they had been just about a year before this present story opens.

The Sherwoods lived in a little cottage on Amity Street in Tillbury. Bess Harley lived with her parents and brothers and sisters in the same town; but they were much better off financially than the Sherwoods. Mr. Sherwood was a foreman in the Atwater Mills, and when that company abruptly closed down, Nan's father was thrown out of work and the prospect of real poverty stared the Sherwoods in the face.

Then the unexpected happened. A distant relative of Mrs. Sherwood's died, leaving her some property in Scotland. But it was necessary for her to appear personally before the Scotch courts to obtain Hughie Blake's fortune.

Circumstances were such, however, that her parents could not take Nan with them. It was a hard blow to the girl; but she was plucky and ready to accept the determination of Momsey and Papa Sherwood. When they started for Scotland, Nan started for Pine Camp with her Uncle Henry, and the first book of this series relates for the most part Nan's exciting adventures in the lumber region of the Michigan Peninsula, under the title of: "Nan Sherwood at Pine Camp; Or, the Old Lumberman's Secret."

As has been mentioned, Nan and her chum, Bess Harley, had come to Lakeview Hall the previous September. The matter of Momsey's fortune had not then been settled in the Scotch courts; but enough money had been advanced to make it possible for Nan to accompany her chum to the very good boarding school on the shore of Lake Huron.

In "Nan Sherwood at Lakeview Hall; Or, the Mystery of the Haunted Boathouse," the two friends are first introduced to boarding-school life, and to this very merry, if somewhat thoughtless, company of girls that have already been brought to the attention of the reader in our present volume.

They were for the most part nice girls and, at heart, kindly intentioned; but Nan had gone through some harsh experiences, as well as exciting times, during the fall and winter semester at Lakeview Hall. She had made friends, as she always did; and the Masons, Grace and Walter, determined to have her with them in Chicago over the holidays. Therefore, in the third volume of the series, "Nan Sherwood's Winter Holidays; Or, Rescuing the Runaways," we find Nan and her chum with their friends in the great city of the Lakes.

During those two weeks of absence from school Nan certainly had experienced some exciting times. Included in her adventures were her experiences in rescuing two foolish country girls who had run away to be motion picture actresses. In addition Nan Sherwood had saved little Inez, a street child, and had taken her back to "the little dwelling in amity," as Papa Sherwood called their Tillbury home. For Nan's parents had returned from across the seas, and she was beginning this second semester at Lakeview Hall in a much happier state of mind in every way than she had begun the first one.

It was only to be expected that Nan would try to make the coming of the girl in brown, Rhoda Hammond, more pleasant than her own first appearance at school had been.

But the girls who had remained at the Hall over the holidays were fairly wild. At least, Mrs. Cupp said so, and Mrs. Cupp, Doctor Beulah Prescott's housekeeper, ought to know for she had had complete charge of the crowd during the intermission of studies.

"And, believe me," sighed Laura Polk, "we've led the dear some dance."

Mrs. Cupp looked very stern now as she suddenly appeared from her office at the end of the big hall. She scarcely responded to the greetings of the girls who had returned—not even to Nan's—but asked in a most forbidding tone:

"Who is there new? Girls who have for the first time arrived, come into my office at once. There is time for the usual formalities before supper."

"Oh, my dear," murmured Bess Harley wickedly, and loud enough for the girl in brown to hear her, "she is in a dreadful temper. She certainly will put these poor sawneys through the wringer tonight."

Rhoda Hammond evidently took this "with a grain of salt." She asked, before going to the office:

"What sort of instrument of torture is the 'wringer,' please?"

"I am speaking in metaphor," explained Bess. "But you wait! She will wring tears from your eyes before she gets through with you. As the little girls say, you can see her 'mad is up.'"

"Oh, now, Elizabeth," warned Nan, "don't scare her."

Rhoda walked away without another word. Bess looked after her with an admiring light in her eyes.

"Oh, Nan! isn't she beautifully dressed?"

"Richly dressed, I agree," said Nan. "But Mrs. Cupp will have something to say about that."

"I know," giggled the wicked and slangy Bess. "She'll give her an earful about dressing 'out of order.' She is worse than Linda."

"No. Better," said Nan confidently. "Whoever chose that girl's outfit showed beautiful taste, even if she is dressed much too richly for the standard of Lakeview Hall."

Linking arms a little later, when the supper gong sounded, the two friends from Tillbury sought the pleasant dining-room where the whole school—"primes" as well as the four upper divisions—ate at long tables, with an instructor in charge of each division.

But discipline was relaxed to-night, as it was always at such times. Even Mrs. Cupp, who, all through the meal, marched up and down the room with a hawk eye on everything and everybody, was less strict than ordinarily.

Nan Sherwood at Rose Ranch

The moment Nan Sherwood appeared the little girls hailed her as their chum and "Big Sister." Nothing would do but she must sit at their table and share their food for this one meal.

"Oh, dear, Nan!" cried one little miss, "did you bring back Beautiful Beulah all safe and sound with you? Shall we have her to play with again this term?"

"Why, bless you, honey!" returned the bigger girl, "I did not even take the doll away. Mrs. Cupp has charge of it, and if she lets me, we will take it up into Room Seven, Corridor Four, to-morrow."

"Oh, won't that be nice?" acclaimed the little girls, for Nan's big doll was an institution at Lakeview Hall among more than the children in the primary department.

But at the end of the meal Nan was dragged away by the older girls. They were an excited and hilarious crowd.

"There's something doing!" whispered Bess in Nan's ear. "That new girl is on our corridor. You know the room that was shut up all last term?"

"Number eight?"

"That is the one. Rhoda has got it. And what do you think?"

"Almost any mischief," replied Nan, with dancing eyes.

"Oh, now, Nan! Well, Laura has told her that the room is haunted. Says a girl died there two years ago and it's never been used since. And so now her ghost will be sure to haunt it—"

"I think that is both mean and silly of Laura," interrupted Nan, with vigor. "She will have some of these little girls, who will be bound to hear the tale, scared half to death. Is that poor girl going to live in Number Eight alone?"

"She is until somebody else comes to mate with her," said Bess carelessly. "Come on, old Poky. We're going to have some fun with that wild Westerner."

"I'll go along," agreed Nan, smiling again, "if only to make sure that you crazy ones do not go too far in your hazing."

CHAPTER III

"CURFEW SHALL NOT RING TONIGHT"

In Corridor Four had always been centered most of Lakeview Hall's "high jinks," to quote Laura Polk. Although Procrastination Boggs, Nan Sherwood, Bess Harley, and several other dwellers on this corridor stood well up in their classes, Mrs. Cupp was inclined to locate most infractions of the school rules in the confines of Corridor Four.

"Our overflowing an-i-mile spirits, young ladies, are our bane," quoted Laura, talking through her nose. "Dr. Beulah has been away—has not arrived home yet—and we unfortunate orphans have been driven to bed with the chickens. I, for one, have revolted."

"You don't look very revolting, Laura," drawled Amelia Boggs, "even with that red necktie on crooked."

"Just the same, I have anarchistic tendencies. I feel 'em," declared the red-haired girl.

"That is not anarchism you feel," scoffed Bess. "If I had eaten what you did for supper—"

"Oh, say not so!" begged Laura. "Don't tell me that all this disturbance within me is from merely what I ate. Why, I feel that I might lead an assault on Cupp's office, take her by force, and immure her in—"

"The old secret passage to the boathouse," put in Nan.

"Oh, goodness—gracious—Agnes!" said Amelia, looking at one of her watches, "if we are going to do anything to that wild Western mustang to-night—"

"Hush! Have no fear," interrupted Laura. "There is time enough."

"Procrastination should know that," giggled Bess, "with all the watches and clocks she owns."

"While we gab here," went on Amelia, "curfew time approaches."

Laura struck an attitude. "Listen, girls!" she cried. "'Curfew shall not ring to-night!'"

"Now, don't begin reciting old chestnuts like that," sniffed Bess.

"It is an announcement of revolt, not a recitation, I'd have you know," declared the red-haired girl.

"What do you mean, Laura?" Nan asked, suddenly seeing that Laura really had some meaning underneath her raillery.

"Hush, children!" crooned the red-haired girl. "What is our greatest trial—our most implacable enemy—in this fair Garden of Eves? Tell me!"

"Mrs. Cupp," sighed Nan.

"Nay, nay! She is but the slave of the lamp," responded Laura, still in flowery fashion. "The *bete noire* of the girls of Lakeview Hall is the half-past nine o'clock curfew. And I vow it shall not ring to-night!"

"Why won't it?" asked Nan, finally grown suspicious.

"Because," hissed Laura, her eyes dancing, "I climbed up into the tower this forenoon and unhooked and hid the bell-clapper. They won't find it for one while, now you mark my word!"

"Oh, Laura!" gasped Nan; but then she, too, had to join in the peal of laughter that the other girls in Room Seven, Corridor Four, emitted.

"What a joke!" exclaimed Bess.

"It's one of those jokes best kept secret," advised Amelia Boggs, who, after all, possessed a fund of caution. "Mrs. Cupp will be desperately moved when she finds it out."

"At least," Nan agreed, "Laura is right. Curfew will not ring to-night. But Mrs. Cupp will find some other way of making it known that retiring hour has arrived. We'd best get to work if we are going to have a procession of the sawneys."

"Girls," suddenly asked Bess, "who ever started that lumberman's slang of 'sawney' for 'greenhorn' up in this hall of acquired good English?"

"Oh, come, Bess!" groaned Amelia, "the term hasn't really opened yet. Don't make us delve into the past for the roots of our language. It's us for the procession now!"

Nan Sherwood entered into the plan for the evening's hazing of newcomers for a special reason. She had liked the girl from the West, Rhoda Hammond, at first sight. Not for her beautiful clothing, but for something Nan had seen in her countenance.

The former purposed to take an active part in whatever was done to the newcomer because she believed she could influence the more thoughtless girls to the extent that nothing very harsh would be done to Rhoda.

"I'll stir up the animals," cried Bess, hopping off her bed, where she had been perching. "We want a big crowd to help worry that Hammond girl."

She was gone in a flash to get together the other girls of Corridor Four. Laura yawned:

"I wonder if we'll be able to worry that wild Western young person much, after all?" she said. "She looked to me like a cool sort of person."

"I don't know," said Amelia. "I think she's stuck up."

"Oh, I wouldn't say that," cried Nan.

"She's dressed to kill, just the same. I'd like to take her for a good long tramp in that outfit she came in."

"Procrastination means this Riotous Rhoda has got too much money—like Linda Riggs," put in Laura.

"I wonder if that Rose Ranch she comes from is a nice place," said Nan. "Just think! A real cattle ranch!"

"Pooh!" said Amelia. "My uncle owns a dairy farm. What's the difference whether you have muley cows or long-horned Texas steers?"

Laura was still chuckling at this when Bess returned with several girls who crowded into the room behind her. There was a busy time for a few minutes as the girls dressed Amelia in an old pillow-slip with eye-holes burned in it, and placed in her hand the staff of a broom, over the brush-end of which was drawn another bag, on which, in charcoal, Grace Mason deftly drew a very wise looking owl in outline.

Thus arrayed, Amelia was to lead the procession and be Mistress of Ceremonies. They were about to start when Laura Polk was suddenly missed.

"Now, where has she gone?" demanded Bess. "She's just like a flea! You put your hand on her, and there she isn't!"

But Laura was back in a moment. She brought with her, and dangled before their wondering gaze, a suit of paint-stained overalls, jumper and all, that evidently by their size belonged to Henry, the boatkeeper and man of all work of Lakeview Hall.

"I hid 'em the other day," declared the red-haired girl. "You never know what may happen, or how such garments as these may come in use."

"But, for pity's sake, Laura!" gasped Nan, "what are they for?"

"Don't they make just the uniform needed for a cowgirl? What say? I bet she rides astride, and these old overalls will remind her of home, at Rustlers' Roost, and all that, you know."

The shrieks of laughter that answered this proposal threatened to bring some of the teachers and so spoil the fun altogether. Finally, however, Amelia Boggs got the crowd into line, and the parade marched out of Room Seven into the corridor.

Room Eight was almost directly opposite the one occupied by Nan and Bess; but Amelia led the procession the full length of the hall and returned again before rapping a summons on Rhoda Hammond's door.

"Oh, yes! In a minute," cried a small voice from inside.

But Amelia waited on no appeal of this character. She found on turning the knob that the door was unlocked. She flung it open and stalked in, the other girls trailing two by two behind her.

"Oh, dear me! what do you want?" gasped Rhoda.

She had removed and hung up in the clothes-closet the beautiful furs, dress, and hat. Her bag was open on the couch, but it seemed to contain no kimono, and the Western girl remained half hidden behind the portiere that hung before the closet.

"What do you want?" she repeated, gazing in wonder at the tall figure of the Mistress of Ceremonies.

"We are just in time," said Amelia behind her mask, and in a supposed-to-be-sepulchral voice. "The sawney is all prepared to don her costume. Hither, slave! and see that she dons the costume quickly, for we must haste."

"The slave hithers," said Laura jovially. "Here you are, Rambunctious Rhoda from Rawhide Springs. Put 'em on."

She held out the overalls and jumper to the surprised new girl, who hesitated to take them.

"*Hic jacet!* The varlet refuses 'em!" hissed the red-haired girl.

"Goodness, Laura," whispered Nan. "That means 'here lies'—and nobody is telling stories."

"She's got her Latin and Shakesperean English most awfully mixed," giggled one of the other girls.

"And 'varlet' is the wrong gender, anyway," observed Bess.

"Silence!" commanded the Mistress of Ceremonies. "Silence in the ranks. Will she not don the costume?"

"Put 'em on!" commanded Laura again, shaking the painter's suit before the hesitating Western girl.

"She would better," said Amelia threateningly, "or I will call to your aid all these, my faithful followers, who have already been through the fiery trial."

"I don't want to go through any fiery trial," said Rhoda. "But if you insist, I'll put on that jacket and the pants."

"'Pants' is truly Western, isn't it, Laura?" asked Amelia Boggs. "Civilized folk say trousers."

"I see I have much to learn," said Rhoda, too meekly, perhaps.

She slipped quickly into the roomy overalls behind the curtain, and then came forth, putting on the jumper. Her bare arms and shoulders were brown and firm. Nan thought Rhoda's figure was as attractive as her face was pretty. She caught the new girl's glance and smiled encouragingly.

"Doesn't she make a darling boy!" whispered Bess Harley to her chum.

But the other girls—at least, some of them—meant to make the newcomer feel keenly her position as a "sawney."

"She wears 'em just as though she was at home in them," said Laura drawlingly. "I tell you she is a regular cowgirl at home on the Hot Dog Mesa. Isn't that so, Miss Rhoda?"

"You seem to know," replied the Western girl bruskly.

Laura suddenly whispered to the hooded Amelia. The latter cleared her throat portentously and said:

"Sawney, it is evident that you must be taught your place. Meekness becomes you lambkins when you first come to Lakeview Hall. Slave, prepare the bandage."

"What's that?" demanded Rhoda. "Do you know, I don't like this foolishness much."

"The fiery trial all right for yours!" exclaimed Laura, who had caught up a towel and was folding it dexterously. "Turn around!"

"I won't!" declared Rhoda flatly.

"Mutiny!" exclaimed Amelia. "Seize the captive and bandage her eyes at once," and she pounded on the floor with the broom handle.

Nan was one of those who grabbed the Western girl. But she did so to whisper swiftly in Rhoda's ear:

"Don't fight against it. It's only fun."

"Fun!" repeated Rhoda in disgust.

But she gave over struggling. Laura blindfolded her quickly and securely. Of course she might have torn the bandage off, for her hands were free. But she waited more calmly now for what might come next.

CHAPTER IV

WALKING THE PLANK

Nan Sherwood knew very well that there was no intention of really injuring the new girl; therefore she made no objection to what was done. Indeed, she helped haze Rhoda Hammond, but more for the sake of seeing that the Western girl was not taken advantage of in any way than for the fun of the prank.

Nan did not know what Amelia and Laura had planned to do to the new girl, but knowing the older girls as well as she did, she was sure that nothing very bad was intended.

Somebody found an old striped silk parasol with some of the panels split, and this was opened and given to Rhoda to carry. The line of march was then taken up, with the victim directly behind the Mistress of Ceremonies and Laura and Nan shutting off all chance of Rhoda's escape.

The latter's cheeks were very red and her teeth gripped her lower lip tightly. Bess mentioned, giggling, that Rhoda looked already as though she were going through the fiery trial!

Nan realized it would have gone much better for the Western girl if she had taken it smiling. She feared that Rhoda's attitude would make the hazing more severe and more prolonged. She wished she knew what was in the minds of Laura and Amelia Boggs regarding the new girl.

The procession marched through Corridor Four to the rear stairway. Amelia stalked ahead, carrying the broom, her "wand of office." The stairway led threateningly near to Mrs. Cupp's room.

"Don't dare breathe even, while we are going down," hissed Laura.

"Silence!" reiterated Amelia.

They descended carefully—all but the prisoner. But when she made too much noise Laura poked her.

"Here!" the red-haired girl muttered, "make believe you are stealing upon a band of Indians to scalp 'em—the poor things! You don't walk like a prairie rose. You stamp along more like a charging buffalo."

"Goodness!" sighed Lillie Nevins, in the rear, "how much our Laura knows about the West, doesn't she?"

At the titter which followed this remark, their leader hissed for silence again. The procession was now winding down the stairway to the rear of Mrs. Cupp's office. They were bound for the basement, it seemed.

For a moment Nan Sherwood wondered if the older girls intended to reach the subterranean passage which connected the trunk room with the boathouse at the foot of the cliff. Then she remembered that the trunk room would be locked at this hour and that Mrs. Cupp had the key.

But the gymnasium was down here, too. The cellars under the school were enormous. Castle-like, the great, rambling building had been constructed by a man with more imagination than money. The latter ran out before his castle on the cliff was completed. After years of emptiness, Dr. Beulah Prescott had obtained it and made it into what it now was—a school for girls.

The great gymnasium was not locked. Laura ran quickly when they entered the dusky place, and punched the light buttons.

"What do you suppose Mrs. Gleason will say?" whispered Grace Mason. Mrs. Gleason was the athletic instructor.

"She won't say a thing if she doesn't know," declared Bess promptly.

Some one closed the door, and Nan saw then that there were at least twenty girls in the room. Some had joined the procession from other corridors. Now they all began to gabble at once, and Amelia pounded frantically for order.

Nan saw that the bandage was sufficiently tight across Rhoda's eyes. Then she led her into the middle of the great room. Amelia was beckoning.

There had been repairs going on in the gymnasium during the holidays, and a good deal of the paraphernalia had been disarranged. It was evident, too, that the workmen were not entirely through. A long plank, used by the men as a scaffolding, stretched from one set of horizontal bars to another on the platform at one end of the room.

Laura called the other girls and in whispers directed them to gather all the mattresses and pile them on the platform under the somewhat insecure plank. Amelia, her eyes sparkling through the holes in the pillow-slip, held Nan and the prisoner back.

"Sawney," the tall girl said sternly, "as you have filed objections to being tried by fire according to the ancient and honorable custom of Lakeview lambkins, you shall be treated as a robber—No! A pirate. You shall be made to walk the plank."

"Well," said Rhoda, rather scornfully. She did not see anything funny in all this.

"It will be a pretty deep well you will plop into," threatened Amelia. "Ready, slaves?"

"Your slaves are slavishly ready," called Laura from the platform. "Let the sawney climb the ship's taffrail and be plunged into the sea."

"We ought to tie her hands behind her," said one girl, as they marched down the room.

"No," said Nan.

"That is right," said Amelia. "We must give her a chance to swim when she strikes the water."

"Oh, fiddlesticks!" murmured Rhoda.

But Nan saw Laura run and fill a big dipper with water from the spigot and give it to one of the other girls, who climbed quickly to the platform. Then Laura came to seize the victim's other arm. She and Nan marched Rhoda, willy-nilly, down the room and up the steps to the platform.

Rhoda stumbled on each step and held her head down. Nan, therefore, judged that Rhoda could see a little from under the bandage. But she did not call Laura's attention to this fact.

"Mount her quickly, slaves!" called Amelia from below. "Force her to walk the plank instantly!"

There had been a stepladder set up against the first horizontal bar set, right at the end of the plank. Nan saw that the mattresses were all in place and that a fall from the plank would only be about three feet. Such a fall was not likely to be serious, and to girls used to athletic drill it seemed a mere nothing. And yet—

"Come on!" commanded Laura, half lifting Rhoda up the stepladder.

"Careful, Laura!" whispered Nan. "If she should fall—"

"Then she will escape drowning," said the red-haired girl, coolly and aloud.

"Fudge!" muttered the victim, who seemed in a very much disgusted mood.

"Beseemeth the candidate is not sufficiently impressed by her situation," hissed Laura.

She and Nan had scrambled up the steps with the blindfolded Rhoda. There was a cross-plank which gave the three uncertain footing.

"Oh, look out!" gasped Nan, wavering herself upon the edge of the plank.

"Hey! We don't want to have to raise the 'man overboard' cry just yet," grumbled Laura. "Easy there, Nancy!"

Nan whispered in Rhoda's ear: "Walk straight ahead. It isn't hard. I'll be ready to catch you."

"Out on the plank, sawney!" commanded Amelia from below.

Laura pushed Rhoda ahead. The candidate for initiation, even if she could see a little from under the bandage, had at best a very uncertain idea of where she was, or where she was going. Besides, with one's eyes practically blinded, it is very difficult indeed to walk a chalk line, even on the floor. And this plank that was far from steady was only about a foot in width.

"Oh!" ejaculated Rhoda, one foot before the other and her arms waving for a balance. The parasol did not help much.

"Oh! oh! oh!" was the prolonged wail from the crowd below.

"You—think—you're—so—smart!" Again the Western girl teetered back and forth. Laura gave her another slight push. Rhoda took one more step, and let the parasol fall.

"Good!" encouraged Nan.

"Treason!" croaked Laura, observing Nan's encouragement of the candidate.

"Have a care, sawney," declared Amelia Boggs sternly. "A false step and you are lost! The ravening sea is below you. Feel the spray dashing in your face!"

Quick as a flash the girl with the dipper filled her palm with water and threw it upward. It spattered into Rhoda's face and she jerked back her head.

The motion destroyed the balance she had gained. She uttered a stifled ejaculation and wavered again. Laura stretched out a hand and wickedly nudged the victim.

"Oh, don't!" yelled Nan, and she leaped down upon the mattresses.

Rhoda completely lost her equilibrium. She uttered another scream and stepped out into space.

"Man overboard!" shouted Laura.

And as Rhoda fell the girl with the dipper flung its contents over the flying figure of the new girl.

CHAPTER V

RHODA IS UNPOPULAR

The blindfolded Rhoda came down so awkwardly that Nan feared she would be hurt. The girl from Tillbury screamed a warning—which was useless.

But in that exciting moment Nan noted something that afterward gave her a sidelight upon Rhoda Hammond's character. As the Western girl felt herself going she snatched off the blindfolding towel.

Self-possession! Rhoda owned that attribute, largely developed. She was cool, if angry.

When she landed on the padded platform, she fell on her knees, and the fall must have jarred her. But she was up in a flash, and the girl with the dipper, Minnie Wolff, found herself in the muscular grasp of Rhoda's arms.

"There, now, I've had enough of this foolishness!" snapped the Western girl, limping toward the platform steps. "I've wrenched my knee, and I should hope you'd be satisfied. I want nothing more to do with your baby plays! I came to Lakeview Hall to study and learn something—"

"Oh, you are going to learn something all right," drawled Laura, interrupting Rhoda's angry speech. "But I can see it is going to take you some time, Miss Rhoda Hammond. You are going to have a nice time here!"

Rhoda pushed through the group of girls with blazing face. Her eyes were hard and dry. She had evidently hurt her knee quite badly, for she could not walk without limping. Nan ran after her.

"Oh, Rhoda, don't take it so," she begged in a whisper. "It will make it so much harder for you."

"I don't care!"

"But you want to be friends with us."

"With those girls?" repeated Rhoda, in scorn. "Not much!"

"Oh, yes, you do. Every one of them is nice."

"They act so."

"They are!" reiterated Nan. "And you made Minnie cry."

"What did she want to throw that water on me for?"

"But it didn't hurt you," Nan pointed out. "You are dressed for it!"

"Yes," snapped Rhoda, looking down at the jumper and overalls. "I look like a silly in these things."

"Well, you don't need to act like a silly," urged Nan, keeping pace with her, as Rhoda left the gymnasium. "You are making it awfully hard for yourself. The girls won't forgive you."

"Forgive me? Well, I like that!" scoffed Rhoda.

"Oh, yes. It was all in fun. We all have to go through some such performance—when we are greenhorns."

"Not for me!" exclaimed the Western girl with emphasis.

Nan was silent for a moment, guiding the new girl through the unfamiliar and only half-lighted passages to the back stairway. Then Nan asked:

"Does your knee hurt?"

"Of course it does."

"I have some lotion in my room. It is good for a sprain, or anything like that. I'll get it for you and you can rub it in well when you go to bed."

"If those girls come around to bother me again—"

"I'm afraid they won't," said Nan, sorrowfully.

"You're *afraid* they won't?"

"Yes. They may let you very much alone. You won't have much fun here."

"Humph! I can flock by myself," said Rhoda, quite cheerfully.

"But you can have so much better times if you are friends with the other girls."

"I don't know about that. I don't like any of them—as far as I've gone. Except you. Out where I come from—at Rose Ranch—there are plenty of Mexican girls and Indian girls who are much more ladylike than this crowd. Why! these girls are savages."

"Oh, no, Rhoda! Not quite that," laughed Nan. "You don't understand. And I am afraid they won't understand you."

"Who wants 'em to?" responded Rhoda Hammond gruffly.

Nan Sherwood took the liniment into Rhoda's room, and when she returned, bringing back the overall suit to be returned to Henry, she found her chum, Bess Harley, in their room, slowly preparing for bed.

"Well! isn't that the greatest girl you ever saw?" exclaimed Bess. "She will have a nice time here—not! And I should think you'd not have anything to do with her, Nan. The other girls won't like it. We're just going to ignore her. A girl who can't take a joke!"

"I shan't have much to do with her until she comes to her senses," Nan admitted. "But I am sorry for her, just the same."

"You'll waste your 'sorry' on that one," laughed Bess.

"Perhaps. But don't you realize, honey, that we came near being just as foolish as Rhoda Hammond when we came here last fall?"

"Oh, nonsense!" ejaculated Bess; but she blushed.

"Think," said Nan, with twinkling eyes. "Don't you remember that shoe-box lunch we brought with us and that the girls made so much sport of? Didn't you get vexed?"

"Oh! Well! Yes, a little," admitted Bess. "But, Nan! I never acted as foolishly as this Rhoda Hammond. Now, did I?"

"No, you did not, my dear," agreed her chum.

But she might honestly have claimed credit for this being a fact. It had been Nan's better sense and her strong influence over her chum that had kept Bess Harley from acting quite as unwisely as Rhoda Hammond was now acting.

"I expect," was all Nan said, however, "that this poor Rhoda is going to have a very unhappy time of it here, unless she changes her attitude."

"Well, she deserves to. She spoiled our fun and she hurt Minnie badly. I suppose she's had no sort of bringing-up, coming right from that wild country."

Nan chuckled. "I wonder! She thinks we lack proper up-bringing. She compares us unfavorably with the Mexican and Indian girls she has been used to out on the ranch from which she comes."

"Good-night!" gasped Bess indignantly, as she plunged into bed.

It did not take a seeress to foretell Rhoda Hammond's unpopularity during the opening days of this term at Lakeview Hall. It seemed that before breakfast the next morning the whole school was buzzing with the story of the doings of the girls of Corridor Four.

That a newcomer should set herself contrary to a custom that had always been honored at the Hall, was considered unpardonable. Even the older girls—seniors and juniors who thought themselves too dignified for such escapades—had merely a sarcastic smile for the new girl from the West. While the little girls—the "primes"— were frankly curious, and could scarcely keep their gaze off Rhoda at meals, or in the main hall at chapel.

The privilege of hazing had seldom been abused by the girls. Dr. Prescott winked at the romps which never really hurt anybody. No girl with "ingrowing dignity," as Amelia Boggs called it, could hope to be happy with her fellows at Lakeview Hall.

"A proper amount of hazing is bound to reduce the size of the sawney's ego," Laura remarked. "This wild Western person has a swelled ego, if ever I saw one. But she shall be let alone, all right, if that is what she is so anxious for."

Nan was, as she said, sorry for Rhoda; but she could do nothing openly to help matters. She would not speak for the Western girl, for she felt that, in justice, Rhoda was in the wrong.

Unlike many of the other girls, however, Nan failed to find anything about Rhoda's character to dislike. Even Linda Riggs was not pleased with the girl from Rose Ranch. The latter girl threatened quite unconsciously to outshine the railroad magnate's daughter in point of dress.

Mrs. Cupp had something to say about that. It was said tartly enough, of course, and Rhoda had to take it before a good-sized party of other girls.

"Where did your mother think you were coming to, Miss Hammond?" Mrs. Cupp demanded when she had looked over the contents of Rhoda's two trunks. "These clothes might be of use if you expected to attend the opera, or appear in society. How absurd to dress a young girl in such garments! Your mother—"

"Please, Mrs. Cupp, do not blame my mother if you think these things are not suitable for me to wear. She is not at—at fault for their selection. They were bought for me by a friend, mostly in Chicago."

"Humph! Your mother should have attended to your being properly dressed. This is a practical school, not a theatrical company, you have come to," snapped Mrs. Cupp, who was always very severe in matters of dress. "Your mother—"

"Don't criticize my mother, please," interrupted Rhoda again, and her voice was sharper. "My—my mother is blind; she could not pick out my clothes."

The statement sponged the smiles from the faces of all the girls within hearing. Unpopular as the Western girl was, the fact she had made public somehow made the other girls taste pity for her for the first time. Bess Harley fairly sobbed when she and Nan got to their room with the piles of their own garments, which Mrs. Cupp had allowed them to take from their trunks.

"It—it's *mean* that she should have a blind mother," cried Bess angrily. "Why, it makes us sorry for her. And she doesn't deserve to be pitied."

"I wonder?" murmured Nan, somewhat moved herself by the incident.

As the days went by, Nan Sherwood wondered more and more about Rhoda Hammond. Was she deserving of some sympathy for her situation in the school or not? Frankly, Nan was puzzled.

Of course Rhoda was being absolutely left out of all the social good times and larks of the girls who should have been her mates. Likewise in classes and in indoor athletics she seemed out of place.

She had been schooled mostly at home, it appeared. Nan understood—although Rhoda did not say as much—that her mother had personally conducted much of her education until the last two years. Then she had had a governess.

The latter seemed to have been an English woman with rather old-fashioned ideas. Rhoda was grounded well in certain branches and densely ignorant in others which Dr. Prescott considered essential.

And in the athletic classes!

"Why, I thought these Western cowgirls were just like boys—that they were even born with an ability to pitch a ball underhand, for instance, which we girls are not," sighed Laura. "And look at that thing! She doesn't know how to do anything right."

"Oh, not as bad as that," said Nan, smiling.

"Stop trying to make excuses for her, Nan Sherwood," commanded the red-haired girl sharply. "I won't have it. She never saw a basketball game before. She can scarcely lift herself waist-high on the parallel bars. Couldn't chin herself five times in succession on the trapeze to save her life. Why! she might as well be her own grandmother, she knows so little about athletics."

"Huh!" added Bess Harley with equal disgust, "I heard her tell Mrs. Gleason she thought such things were only for boys. She's a regular sissy!" But this made her hearers laugh.

Nan joined in the laughter, but she added:

"You get into a wrestling match with her and see if she's a sissy. She has developed her muscles by other means than gymnasium tricks. She is so very wiry and strong—you have no idea!"

"But she walks so funny," remarked Lillie Nevins.

"Perhaps that is because she has walked so little," said Nan, wisely.

"Humph!" Amelia Boggs commented, "has she been used to being pushed in a baby carriage?"

"Distances are long out in the cattle country. Everybody rides, I guess," Nan observed.

"Well," one of the older girls remarked, "she's no material for basketball, or any other team. She can't even run, it seems. I guess we'll have to pass her up."

Nor did Rhoda seem to mind being "passed up." At least, if she missed the companionship of her schoolmates, she did not show it. Perhaps Nan Sherwood worried more about Rhoda than Rhoda did about herself.

There came a day, however, when the girls of Lakeview Hall saw something in the girl from Rose Ranch that they were bound to admire. Rhoda Hammond possessed one faculty that raised her, head and shoulders, above most of her schoolmates who so derided her.

CHAPTER VI

THE MEXICAN GIRL

The schoolwork was in full swing by this time, and almost every girl seemed to be doing well. "Dr. Beulah," as her pupils lovingly called the head of the school (though not, of course, to her face), went about with a smile most of the time; and even Mrs. Cupp was less grim than usual.

There was an early January thaw that spoiled all outdoor sport for the Lakeview Hall girls. Skating, bobsledding, skiing, and even walking, was taboo for a while, for there was more mud in sight than snow. The girls had to look for entertainment on Saturday in other directions.

Therefore it was considered a real godsend by the girls of Corridor Four when Lillie Nevins told them of the new shop at Adminster. Adminster was about ten miles from Freeling, the little town under the cliff, where the Lakeview Hall girls usually shopped.

"It must be a delightfully funny store," said the flaxen-haired Lillie. "It's full of those Indian blankets, and bead-trimmed things, and Mexican drawn-work, and pottery. Oh! ancient pots and pitchers—"

"Made last year in New Jersey?" scoffed Laura Polk.

"No, no! These are real Mexican. Doctor Larry's girls told me about it. They have been over there and bought the loveliest things!"

There was a good deal of talk about this. It was at the supper table. Nan and Bess were just as much interested as the other girls, and they determined to go to the Mexican curio shop if they could obtain permission.

Nan noticed that for once Rhoda seemed interested in what the other girls were saying. Her brown eyes sparkled and a little color came and went in her cheeks as the discussion went on.

The girl from Tillbury was tempted to invite Rhoda to go with her on Saturday. Yet she felt that Rhoda was not in a mood to accept any overture of peace. The Western girl treated Nan herself well enough;

but Nan could not offend her older friends by showing Rhoda Hammond many favors.

So many of the girls asked permission to visit Adminster on the next Saturday afternoon that Mrs. Cupp allowed Miss March, one of the younger instructors and a favorite of the girls, to accompany them.

It was quite a party that picked its way down the muddy track into Freeling's Main Street where the interurban trolley car passed through toward Adminster. The girls under Miss March's care all but filled the car when it came along; but they were hardly settled when they spied Rhoda Hammond already sitting in a corner by herself.

"Why, Rhoda," said Miss March, rising and going to the Western girl as the car started, "I did not get your name as one of my party."

"No, Miss March," said Rhoda coolly.

"Did you obtain permission to leave the school premises? That is a rule, you know."

"Yes, Miss March," said Rhoda, "I obtained permission."

"From whom, Rhoda?" asked the instructor, rather puzzled.

"I telegraphed yesterday to my father. He sent a night letter to Dr. Prescott, and she got it this morning. She gave it to me. Here it is," said the Western girl, taking the crumpled message from her handbag and handing it to the teacher.

Miss March looked amazed when she had read the long message. "Dr. Prescott, then, granted you this privilege which he asks here?"

"Yes, Miss March," said Rhoda coldly, and Miss March went back to her seat.

"Did you ever?" gasped Bess to Nan and Laura. "Why, it must have cost five dollars or more to telegraph back and forth."

"Humph! she certainly doesn't know the value of money," commented Laura. "She is more recklessly extravagant than Linda."

The rest of the girls paid no further attention to Rhoda. They were having too good a time among themselves. As there were few other passengers on that car to Adminster, the Lakeview Hall pupils came very near to taking charge of it. The conductor was good-natured, and the girls' fun was kept in bounds by Miss March.

All the time the Western girl sat in her corner and looked out of the front window at the dreary landscape. It seemed too bad, Nan Sherwood thought more than once, that Rhoda should have allowed herself to become so frankly ignored by her schoolmates.

Nan missed her when the crowd got out of the car in Adminster. This was a larger town than Freeling, and it was on the main railroad line instead of a branch line, as Freeling was. But at that, Adminster was not very metropolitan.

However, the stores fronting on the main street were rather attractive shops. Bess and Grace, with Nan herself, had some things to buy in the department store which was the town's chief emporium, and they separated for a while from the rest of the party.

But when the trio entered the Mexican shop, which was on a side street, there was the whole party of their schoolmates under Miss March's charge.

Some of the girls had already made purchases, and all were excited over certain finds they had made in the stock. Like all such stores that are established for a few months only, and move from town to town, there was much trash exhibited together with some really worth while merchandise from the Southwest.

Not all of the girls knew how to select the good from the trashy merchandise. There were a man, a woman, and a young girl who waited on the customers, all dressed in Mexican costumes; they were too wise to interfere much with the selections of the customers in any department.

The young girl came forward to meet Nan and her companions, courteously offering her services in showing any goods they might wish to look at Nan shrewdly suspected the man and woman to be Jews; but this girl, with her large, black eyes, raven hair, and flashing white teeth, was undoubtedly a Mexican. She was very pretty.

"I can show what dhe yoong ladies want—yes?" she inquired with a most disarming smile.

"Oh, we want to look about, first of all," cried Bess. "Look at all those blankets, Nan! What bully things to throw over our couch!"

"And that lovely spread!" cried Grace.

They went from one lot of goods to another.

The Mexican girl, smiling and quite enjoying their comments, strolled after them. Nan turned to ask her a question regarding a beaded cloth that was evidently meant for a table-scarf. And at the moment Rhoda Hammond entered the shop.

The saleswoman was nearest and she turned to welcome the Western girl. But Nan saw that the girl who was waiting on her started as though to approach the newcomer. Then she stopped, and under her breath hissed an exclamation that must have been in Spanish.

The girl's eyes blazed, her black brows drew together, and she gave every indication of an excitement that was originated by anger. It could be nothing else!

Rhoda Hammond was perfectly unconscious of either the Mexican girl's attention, or her emotion. With the saleswoman who had come to wait on her the girl from Rose Ranch was discussing the price of a piece of pottery which had attracted her notice.

Suddenly the Mexican girl turned to see Nan Sherwood staring at her in wonder. She flushed darkly and was at first inclined to turn away. Then her excitement overpowered her natural caution. She seized Nan by the wrist with a pressure of her fingers that actually hurt.

"You know all dhese yoong ladies—yes?" she demanded. "Dhey all coom wit' you? Huh?"

"Why, yes. We all come from the same school," admitted the astonished Nan.

"You know dhat girl?" asked the Mexican, pointing quickly at Rhoda.

"Yes."

"She do go to school wit' you all—yes? Her name?" demanded the other.

"Why—"

"Eet ees Ham-mon'—no?" hissed the strangely acting girl. "Senorita Ham-mon'?"

"Her name is Hammond. Yes. Rhoda Hammond," admitted Nan, scarcely knowing whether it was right to tell the girl this fact or not.

"Ah, eet ees so! Senorita Ham-mon', of dhe Ranchio Rose. Huh?"

"Why—why—" gasped Nan. "Yes, her home is at Rose Ranch. That is what she calls it."

"Ah!" hissed the Mexican girl, her eyes still glittering angrily. "See! See how reech she is dress'. Huh! The treasure of Ranchio Rose buy dhose dress'. Huh! Ah!"

She flung herself about and walked hastily to the back of the store. Nan was speechless. She stood utterly amazed by the Mexican girl's words and actions.

CHAPTER VII

DOWN THE SLOPE

Nobody seemed to have noticed the strange actions of the Mexican girl save Nan—least of all Rhoda herself. There was no time to speak of the incident while they remained in the shop, even had Nan decided that it was best to do so.

The Mexican girl did not reappear from the rear of the shop. The girls all bought something—perhaps not wisely in every case. Nan Sherwood saw a queer smile on Rhoda Hammond's face as she noted some of the trinkets the other girls purchased. Of course, the girl from Rose Ranch could have advised them about the real value of these articles. But who would ask her?

It really was too bad. Most of the crowd ignored Rhoda Hammond altogether. They did not even speak to her when they brushed her furs in passing.

Rhoda was beautifully dressed, and Bess audibly wondered who had purchased Rhoda's clothes, as her mother's affliction made it impossible for her to have selected them.

The Western girl left the store before the others had finished shopping and Nan fancied Rhoda intended to catch an earlier car back to Freeling than the one Miss March and her party were to take. Nan said nothing to Bess or to Grace regarding the peculiar actions of the Mexican girl who had evidently recognized Rhoda, and knew where she came from. Nan was enormously interested in the mystery; but she did not think it was right to make common property of what she had seen or heard. She was the more tempted to go to Rhoda herself and ask about it.

Perhaps it was something that Rhoda really ought to know. The Mexican girl had looked at the unnoticing Rhoda in a very angry way. And she had spoken very strangely.

"The treasure of the Ranchio Rose buy those dresses."

That was a very peculiar way to have spoken, to say the least. What was "the treasure of Rose Ranch?" Nan was very desirous of asking Rhoda Hammond to explain.

Of course she could not make the inquiry without telling Rhoda about the Mexican girl. Nan wondered if that would be a wise thing to do. Rhoda had not appeared to notice the strange girl. Had she done so, would she have recognized the Mexican as the latter had her?

All the time these thoughts and queries were rioting in Nan Sherwood's mind she had to give her open attention to the buying of certain articles and to the questions and observations of the other girls. She and Bess purchased several things for their room; but Nan would have been better satisfied if they had been intimate enough with Rhoda to have asked her advice about the purchases.

They all trooped out with their bundles at last.

"My goodness!" laughed Bess, "we look like a gang of Italian immigrants being taken by a padrone into the woods. Only we should wear shawls over our heads instead of hats."

They went merrily along the streets to the point from which the car for Freeling started, and lo! there was Rhoda Hammond. She had evidently missed the previous car.

"Is that girl going to tag us wherever we go?" Bess asked, with some vexation.

"Sh!" warned Grace. "She has a perfect right to come over here to Adminster, of course."

"My goodness! I should say she has," Lillie Nevins said, laughing. "After telegraphing to her father for permission."

When the car came along Rhoda got in at the front and took the corner seat again, while the others crowded in through the rear door. The old man who acted as motorman was well known to some of the girls, and they hailed him, as well as the conductor, gayly. But the motorman seemed in no pleasant mood, for he scarcely answered their sallies.

He shut himself into the forward platform before the conductor gave the signal for starting, and dropped the latch on the double doors so that the girls should not disturb him. When the conductor took up the fares he said, on being questioned by Laura Polk:

"Oh, John is not feeling well, I guess. He hasn't acted like himself all day. But it's as much as my life's worth to ask him how he feels. He's got the temper of a wolf when he's under the weather—poor old John has."

Of course, the girls gave the motorman little attention—unless Rhoda did from her situation up front. The rest of them only noticed him when he started or stopped the car with more than ordinary abruptness.

"I do wish he wouldn't jerk the car so," complained Laura Polk. "He's made me almost swallow my gum twice."

"Gracious, Laura!" gasped Lillie Nevins, looking alarmed, "if you really have any gum you had better swallow it before Miss March sees you."

At this Laura merely chuckled delightedly.

"I really don't like the way this man is running the car," Miss March said finally to the conductor. "Tell him to have a care. He will have us off the track."

The interurban line was not a smooth, straight-ahead road. They swung around turns that were somewhat sharp. John stormed along as though he were running on a perfectly straight track.

"I'll see what I can do," said the conductor doubtfully, and he went forward and tapped on the glass of the front door. But the motorman only gave him an angry glance and would not even reach around and lift the latch.

"He's running away with us!" exclaimed Lillie Nevins, who was always easily frightened.

"Oh, my dear!" laughed another girl. "What an elopement!"

"I hate to do it," said the conductor, when he came back to Miss March. "But I'll report him to the inspector when we get to the end of the route."

The car topped the heights of the ridge of hills that lay between Adminster and Freeling. On the Freeling side of the ridge the slope to the valley was almost continuous. But near the bottom was a sharp curve. Here was a low stone wall along the edge of the road, beyond which was a sheer drop of thirty or more feet into a rocky gorge. It was a perilous spot. More than one accident had happened there; but never an electric car accident.

The rapidity with which the motorman ran the car, and the jerky way in which he stopped and started it, did not bother Nan Sherwood much, for she was not nervous. Miss March, however, began to stare ahead apprehensively, and the way in which she twisted her pocket-handkerchief in her hands as the car started down the long slope betrayed her feelings. Nan was really sorry for Miss March.

The wheels pounded over the rail-joints and the car began to rock threateningly. A small obstruction on the track would very likely have thrown the car off the rails.

"I do wish that man would have a care," sighed Miss March.

Nan jumped up. She feared that the teacher would soon become hysterical. Also, Grace and Lillie began to betray fear and more of the girls were anxious. Nan stumbled forward to the end of the car. Rhoda sat there, looking ahead, and betraying no emotion at all.

Nan could see the shoulders of the motorman, who was sitting on the one-legged stool on which he had a right to rest when the car was out of town. The rules of the company did not force him to stand all the time. His head seemed to sag forward on his breast. The car was running so fast that he pitched from side to side on his seat—

Or was it from some other reason that his body swayed so? The question shocked Nan Sherwood.

"Oh, Rhoda!" she exclaimed, turning to the Western girl, "what is the matter with him?"

Rhoda Hammond sprang up. Her face was pale but her lips were firmly compressed. She clung to the handle of the door. Nan was holding herself upright by clinging to the other handle.

"There is something the matter with that man!" cried the girl from Tillbury.

They shook the door handles. Of course they could not open the door, nor did the motorman heed them in any way.

Nan screamed aloud then. She saw the hands of the man slip from the handle of the brake and from the controller. The car seemed to leap ahead, gaining additional speed. The man slipped sideways from his stool and crumpled on the platform of the car.

The other girls did not see this. Even the conductor on the rear platform did not know what had happened. Only Nan and Rhoda realized fully the trouble.

"My dear!" gasped Nan, "we cannot get to him. And nobody can stop the car!"

She felt almost a sensation of nausea at the pit of her stomach. She did not weep or lose control of herself. But she felt frightfully helpless.

There seemed nothing to do but to stand there, clinging to the door handle, and watch the car reeling down the slope at a speed that promised disaster at the curve, if not before. Never in her life, in any time of emergency, had Nan Sherwood felt so utterly helpless.

The girl from the West said not a word. She, too, clung to the handle and stared through the pane at the crumpled figure of the motorman on the platform. But she remained thus only for a moment.

Suddenly she swung sideways and pushed Nan away from the door. The latter tumbled into the nearest seat. Hanging by her left hand to the door handle, Rhoda Hammond doubled her gloved right and smashed one of the glass panes in the door.

At the crash of glass Nan sprang to Rhoda's side, and everybody screamed. The conductor burst open the rear door and started forward. Rhoda paid no attention to the shouts behind her.

She reached through the broken pane and lifted the latch which held the two halves of the door together. She flung them apart and leaped down the single step to the enclosed front platform of the car, Nan close at her side.

The conductor arrived. But it was the girl from Rose Ranch who did it all. She seized the controller and turned off the current. Her right hand wound up the brake as though she had practiced the work. Fast as the car was speeding, the pressure on the wheels made itself felt almost at once. Nan wished to help, but realized that in her ignorance she might blunder, so held herself in.

"What's happened to John?" demanded the conductor. "My goodness!" he added to Rhoda, "you're a smart girl."

But he took her place at the brake. The car did not halt at once. It ran down almost to the turn in the road before it came to a jarring halt.

Some of the frightened girls had gathered around Miss March. The others crowded forward. Nan was holding Rhoda Hammond tight about the neck, and she kissed her warmly.

"You are a splendid girl, Rhoda!" Nan cried. "You stopped the car."

"I didn't see that you showed any white feather, Nan," urged Bess Harley.

"Ah, but Rhoda was more than brave. She knew what to do. We'd have gone off the track and pitched over that wall probably, if it had depended on me to stop this old car," declared Nan generously.

CHAPTER VIII

AFTERNOON TEA

The girls from Lakeview Hall were not likely to forget their experience on the car for many a long day. And they were honestly appreciative of the fact that Rhoda Hammond, the girl from Rose Ranch, had saved their lives.

But they did not really know how to show Rhoda that, in spite of her bad start at the Hall, the attitude of at least the party of girls who had been with her in the electric car, had changed toward her.

Nan put her arms about the Western girl and kissed her warmly. She could do that, for from the start she had been kind to the girl from Rose Ranch. But the others hesitated. Rhoda was not a shallow girl. She did not turn easily from one attitude to another.

The unconscious motorman had been picked up and laid on a seat in the car, and the conductor had run them into Freeling. John was there put in a hospital ambulance. That was all they could do for him.

The doctors said he had been walking around suffering from pneumonia for several days. The girls sent him flowers and some other luxuries and comforts when he was better.

But what could they do for Rhoda?

"I don't think we had better try to do anything *for* her," Nan finally said, after suggestions had been discussed ranging from presenting Rhoda with a gold medal to falling down on their knees and begging her forgiveness.

"We have nothing really to ask her pardon for. It actually was her own stupidity that made her begin so unfortunately among us. She, perhaps, can't see that. Or, if she does, she is too obstinate to admit it."

"Why, Nan!" cried warm-hearted Bess Harley, who, once moved in the right direction, could not do too much for the object of her approval. "Why, Nan! you speak as though you did not like Rhoda, after all. You are the only one who stood up for her all those weeks."

"When did I stand up for her?" demanded Nan. "I would not treat her unkindly. But I have thought all the time she was in the wrong. And there is no use going to Rhoda and telling her we were wrong and that we are sorry. That would not only be a falsehood, but it would do no lasting good."

"Hear! Hear!" cried Amelia. "Minerva Sherwood speaks."

"I guess Nan has got the 'wise' of it," agreed Laura. "No matter how well we may think of Rhoda, she would be equally offended if we all suddenly changed toward her in a way to make her conspicuous. We must begin treating her naturally."

"That's all right," agreed Amelia. "But we cannot overlook the incident of that car ride."

"I should say not!" exclaimed Bess Harley.

"Everybody is talking about it," said Grace.

"Dr. Beulah spoke of it this morning at chapel," Lillie said, "although she did not mention Rhoda's name."

"But everybody knew who she meant," Bess declared.

"For that she can thank Miss March," laughed Laura. "She will never get over talking about Rhoda's bravery."

"And poor Rhoda looked scared in chapel," said Nan. "She thought she was going to be publicly commended for what she had done," and Nan finished with laughter.

"Well," cried Bess, "what shall we do, girls?"

"No," Nan said once more with gravity, "that isn't it. It's what will she do? That is the question. Let Rhoda meet us half way, at least. Otherwise we'll all be stiff and formal and never get any nearer to that wild Western girl than before. I'll tell you!"

"Go ahead. That's what we are waiting for. Tell us," begged Laura.

They gathered closer about the girl from Tillbury and Nan lowered her voice while she explained her idea. So the girls of Corridor

Four—at least, all those who had been aboard the electric car when Rhoda's self-possession had saved them from disaster—were merely courteous to the girl from Rose Ranch, or smiled at her when they met, and kept deftly away from the exciting adventure in their conversation while Rhoda was near.

Apparently the afternoon tea was given in Room Seven in honor of Beautiful Beulah, Nan's famous doll.

"But I'm too big to play dolls," Rhoda Hammond objected when Nan urged her attendance on a rainy Saturday afternoon.

"Pshaw!" laughed Nan, "you're not too big to pass tea and cocoa and sweet crackers to the primes who will come to worship at the shrine of my Beautiful Beulah. That's what I want you for—to help. Bess and I can't do it all."

It was hard to refuse Nan Sherwood anything.

"Laura declares one has to be real mad at you to get out of anything you want us to do!" complained Bess one day, when yielding to Nan's pressure and doing something she would have preferred not to do.

These "doll-teas" in Number Seven, Corridor Four, had become very popular toward the latter end of the previous term at Lakeview Hall. Every girl in the school—even the seniors and juniors—knew of Beautiful Beulah, and the little girls in the primary department flocked to Nan Sherwood's parties whenever they had the chance, bringing their own dolls.

On this particular occasion, however, the young girls came early, were "primed" (as Laura said) with goodies and cocoa, and sent away; the older girls, dropping in one by one, were huddled on beds, chairs, the couch, and even sat Turk-fashion on the floor, gradually filling the room. The crowd included all those girls who had gone to Adminster two Saturdays previous.

Nan had kept Rhoda so busy helping behind the tea table that the Western girl did not realize at once how the character of the party had changed. And shrewd Nan had got Rhoda to talking, too.

A query or two about Rose Ranch, something about the Navaho blanket Nan and her chum had bought for their couch—before she knew it the girl from the West was eagerly describing her home, and telling more in ten minutes about her life before she had come to Lakeview Hall than she had related to anybody in all the weeks she had been here.

"Rose Ranch must be a great place," sighed Bess longingly.

"A beautiful country?" suggested Amelia.

"Magnificent views all around us," Rhoda agreed softly. "A range of hills to the southeast that we call the Blue Buttes. Many mesas on their tops, you know, on which the ancient Indian peoples used to till their gardens. There was a city of Cliff Dwellers not fifty miles from our house."

"Sounds awf'ly interesting," declared Laura.

"And winding through the Blue Buttes is the old Spanish Trail. Up from Mexico by that trail came the Spanish Conquistadors, they say," Rhoda went on, quite excited herself now, in telling of her home and its surroundings.

"And I s'pose there's an electric car line running through those hills now—on the Spanish Trail, I mean?" laughed Laura.

"Well, no. We're not quite as far advanced as that," the Western girl said, good-naturedly enough. "But we don't have any Indian scares nowadays. The Indians used to ride through that gap in the Blue Buttes years ago. Now it's only Mexican bandits."

"Never!" gasped Bess, sitting up suddenly.

"You don't mean it?" from Grace and Lillie in unison.

"You're just spoofing us, aren't you, Rhoda?" drawled Amelia Boggs.

"No, no. We do have Mexican bandits. There is Lobarto. He is no myth."

"Fancy!" exclaimed one of the other girls. "A live bandit!"

"Very much so," said Rhoda. "He has made us a lot of trouble, this Lobarto; although it has been six years since he came into our neighborhood last. He drove off a band of father's horses at that time. But our boys got after him so quick and chased him so hard that they say he took less back to Mexico with him than be brought over the border."

"What does that mean?" asked Bess quickly.

"Why, he brought with him a lot of plunder, they say," Rhoda explained, "and he could not carry it back."

"Then your folks got the plunder?" inquired Nan.

"Not exactly! Lobarto hid it. But our boys got back the horses. And they killed several of Lobarto's gang."

"Mercy! Just listen to her!" cried Laura excitedly. "Why! I was just making believe about your coming from the wild and woolly West; and you really do!"

"Not very woolly around Rose Ranch," said Rhoda grimly. "Father does not approve of sheep. The nesters make us trouble enough, without having sheepmen."

"What are 'nesters'?" asked Amelia.

"I guess you'd call 'em 'squatters' farther East. We don't like them on the ranges. They are small farmers who come and take up quarter sections of the open lands and fence them in."

"But is there really a treasure buried on Rose Ranch?" asked Nan, much more interested in this than she wished the others to observe.

"Why, I suppose so. They all say so. Lobarto and his gang were run off so quick that he had to cache almost everything but the hard cash he had with him. He had raided two churches in Mexico and plundered several haciendas before coming up from the Border, so people say."

"Why don't you ranch folks go and dig up his loot?" demanded Bess, wide-eyed.

"Well," laughed Rhoda, "we don't know where it is cached. It sounds rather preposterous, too—a wagon-load of gold and silver plate, altar ornaments, candlesticks, jeweled cloths, and all that. It does sound sort of romantic, doesn't it?"

"I should say it did!" the girls chorused.

Nan did not say another word in comment at the time. She was enormously curious about what she had overheard the Mexican girl say in the shop at Adminster. And how strangely she had stared at Rhoda Hammond!

CHAPTER IX

NOT ALWAYS "BUTTERFINGERS"

Following that afternoon tea matters changed for Rhoda Hammond at Lakeview Hall. Nor did she overlook Nan's part in bringing her into the social life of the girls whom she met in classes and at the table.

At her books Rhoda was neither brilliant nor dull. She was just a good, ordinary student who stood well enough in her classes to satisfy Dr. Prescott. In athletics, however, Rhoda did not reach a high mark.

In the first place she could not see the value of all the gymnasium exercises; and the indoor games did not interest her much. She was an outdoors girl herself, and had stored up such immense vitality and was so muscular and wiry that she possibly did not need the exercises that Mrs. Gleason insisted upon.

They tried Rhoda at basketball, and she proved to be a regular "butterfingers." Laura, who captained one of the scrub teams, tried to make something of her, but gave it up in exasperation.

Nan, Bess, and Amelia took Rhoda to the basement tennis court and did their best to teach her tennis. She learned the game quickly enough; but to her it was only "play."

"She hasn't a drop of sporting blood in her," groaned Bess. "It seems just silly to her. It is something to pass away the time. Batting a little ball about with a snowshoe, she calls it! And if she misses a stroke, why, she lumbers after the ball like that bear we saw in the Chicago Zoo, Nan, that chased snowballs. 'Member?"

"Well, I never!" laughed Nan. "Rhoda's no bear."

"But she surely is a 'butterfingers,'" Amelia said. "No fun in her at all."

"Says she doesn't see any reason for getting in a perspiration running down here, when she might be using her spare time upstairs reading a book, or knitting that sweater for Nan's Beautiful Beulah."

So, after all, Rhoda Hammond did not become very popular with her schoolmates during those two long and dreary months, February and March, when outdoor exercise was almost impossible in the locality of Lakeview Hall.

Best of all, Rhoda liked to sit in Number Seven, Corridor Four, with Nan and Bess and others who might drop in and talk. If Rhoda herself talked, it was almost always about Rose Ranch. Sometimes about her mother, though she did not often speak of Mrs. Hammond's affliction.

To Nan, Rhoda had once said her mother had been a school-teacher who had gone from the East to the vicinity of the Mexican Border to conduct a school. Her eyes had been failing then; and the change of climate, of course, had not benefited her vision.

"Daddy Hammond," said Rhoda, speaking lovingly of her father, "is twenty years older than mother; but he was so kind and good to her, I guess, when she had to give up teaching, that she just fell in love with him. You know, I fell in love with him myself when I got big enough to know how good he was," and she laughed softly.

"You see, he knows me a whole lot better than mother does, for she has never seen me."

"Doesn't that sound funny!" gasped Nan. "Fancy! Your own mother never having seen you, Rhoda!"

"Only with her fingers," sighed Rhoda. "But mother says she has ten eyes to our two apiece. She 'sees' with the end of every finger and thumb. It is quite wonderful how much she learns about things by just touching them. And she rides as bravely as though she had her sight."

"My!" exclaimed Nan, with a little shudder. "It would scare me to see her."

"Oh, she rides a horse that is perfectly safe. Old Cherrypie seems to know she can't see and that he has to be extremely careful of her."

It was when Rhoda told more about the ranch, however—of the bands of half-wild horses, the herds of shorthorns, the scenery all about her home, the acres upon acres of wild roses in the near-by canyons, the rugged gulches and patches of desert on which nothing but cacti grew, the high mesas that were Nature's garden-spots—that Nan Sherwood was stirred most deeply.

"I think it must be a most lovely place, that Rose Ranch!" she cried on one occasion.

"It is a lovely place; and I'd dearly love to have you see it, Nan Sherwood. You must go home with me when school is over. Oh, what a lark! That would be just scrumptious, as Bess says."

"Oh, it is too long a journey. I never could go so far," Nan said, wistfully it must be confessed.

But Rhoda nodded with confidence. "Oh, yes, you could," she declared. "You spent your Christmas holidays in Chicago with Grace. And before that, you say, you went up to a lumber camp in Michigan. One journey is no worse than another—only that to Rose Ranch is a little longer."

"A *little* longer!"

"Well, comparatively. To going to China, for instance," laughed Rhoda. "Of course you can go home with me."

But Nan laughed at that cool statement. She was quite sure Momsey and Papa Sherwood would veto any such wild plan. And she had been away so much from them during the past year. But she received fine reports regarding her mother's health and Papa Sherwood's new automobile business; and little Inez, under Momsey's tuition, was beginning to write brief, scrawly notes to Nan to tell her how happy she was in the little dwelling in amity.

Winter could not linger in the lap of spring for ever. The snow under the hedges disappeared almost over night. The mud of the highways dried up.

The sparkling surface of the lake was ruffled temptingly by the light breezes and drew the girls of Lakeview Hall boatward. The outdoor tennis courts, the croquet grounds, the basketball enclosure, and the cinder track were put into shape for the season. The girls buzzed outside the Hall like bees about a hive at swarming time.

Grace Mason took up horseback riding again. Her father and mother were still at their town house, but her brother Walter and his tutor were at the summer home a short distance from Lakeview Hall, where he was "plugging," as he called it, for the entrance examinations of a college preparatory school in the fall.

Walter had been unable to be much with his sister since the holidays; but now he came for Grace three times a week to accompany her on her rides.

He bestrode his own big black horse, Prince, leading the speckled pony Grace was to ride. The pony was a nervous, excitable creature. Rhoda, seeing it for the first time, asked Nan:

"Is Grace Mason used to that creature?"

"I don't know. I never saw it before. But the pony can't be any worse than the big black horse that Walter rides."

"Why, what is the matter with him?" asked the Western girl.

"Prince is so high-spirited. You never know what he is going to do."

"I guess the black horse is spirited; but that is not a fault," Rhoda said. "He looks all right to me. But that little flea-bitten grey is a tricky one. You can tell that. See how her eyes roll."

"Do you think the pony will bite?" asked Lillie Nevins, Grace's chum, who overheard the girl from Rose Ranch.

"Goodness! I should hope so. She's got teeth," laughed Rhoda. "But I mean that probably she is skittish—will shy at the least little thing. And perhaps she will run away if she gets the chance."

"Then I shouldn't think Walter would leave them there alone beside the road," Nan said thoughtfully.

"Reckon he trusts that black horse to stand. He's looped the reins of the grey over the pommel of his own saddle. And that's not a smart trick," added Rhoda.

"Why don't you get a horse and ride with them, Rhoda?" asked Bess Harley. "I guess you just ache to get on that pony?"

"What! Side-saddle?" gasped the girl from Rose Ranch. "I wouldn't risk my neck that way."

Suddenly somebody batted a determined tennis ball from far down the nearest court. It whizzed over the back stop, and—bang!—hit the grey pony on the nose.

Rhoda had not been a bad prophet. The pony with the rolling eye leaped and snorted, all four feet in the air at once, and just as crazy in an instant as ever a horse could be.

But perhaps a much better trained and better-tempered animal would have done the same. She jerked the loop of her bridle-rein off Prince's saddlehorn in that first jump. Then she was away like the wind, her little hoofs spurning the gravel of the path that crossed the school's athletic field and led to the broad steps that led down the face of the cliff to the boathouse and cove.

Mad as the pony was, she might have cast herself down the steep flight. Frightened animals have done such things upon less provocation.

The girls screamed, and that only lent wings to the grey's flying hoofs. But the horror and wild despair of the group at the edge of the field were not caused by the mere running away of the grey pony.

The mad creature was headed for the brink of the cliff; but between the pony and that side of the field was a group of the smaller girls at play. There were almost thirty of the little girls of the Hall engaged in a game of tag, and utterly oblivious to the drumming hoofs of the pony!

The girls did not instantly see the pony coming. And when they did realize their peril they milled for a minute right in her track like a herd of frightened cattle.

Scarcely had the pony started from the road, however, and the peril of the girls become apparent, when Rhoda Hammond leaped into action, jumping to the back of Walter Mason's pawing black Prince.

The girl from Rose Ranch seemed to reach the saddle in a single spring. She was astride the snorting horse and her feet instinctively sought the stirrups, as Prince leaped away in the track of the grey pony.

The stirrup-leathers were longer than Rhoda was used to; for most Western riders use a shorter leather than was the custom about Lakeview Hall. But, almost standing erect as Prince thundered across the athletic field, Rhoda seemed perfectly poised both in body and mind. To see her, one would never suppose that it was possible to fall out of a saddle.

The big black horse seemed to know just what was expected of him. He scarcely needed guiding. The girl's hair snapped out behind her in the wind; her set face, visible to a few of the spectators, gave them confidence. She was no "butterfingers" now. She was going to do what she had set out to do—no doubt of that!

She rode slightly stooping forward from the waist, with left hand outstretched while Prince's reins were gathered loosely in her right hand. The shrieking children were huddled right before the grey pony. It did seem as though they could not possibly escape being trampled upon.

But the stride of the big black horse was almost twice the length of the pony's. And he answered the rein perfectly. Rhoda rode to the right of the grey, stretched forward her long arm, and swerved her own mount at the same moment.

A single jerk on the lines of the pony, dragging her sideways, and the runaway crossed her forefeet and crashed to the ground, almost throwing a somersault the fall was so abrupt.

But the grey was not much hurt. Rhoda had drawn Prince in, was out of the saddle, had run to seize the pony's bridle before the fallen animal could get to her feet and continue her mad race.

CHAPTER X

THE TREASURE OF ROSE RANCH

Walter Mason came running as hard as he could across the field; but he had only to seize Prince's reins and manage that excited animal. Rhoda had the grey pony well in hand.

"Well, you're a wonder for a girl!" exclaimed Grace's brother.

"Humph!" said Rhoda in return, "I don't consider that a compliment—if you meant it as such. Look out, or that black horse will step on you."

"She was just as cool as a cucumber," Walter told Nan and his sister afterward. "Why! I never saw such a girl."

"I guess," Nan Sherwood said shrewdly, "that we don't know much about girls who are born and brought up in the far West. Rhoda Hammond is a friend to be proud of. She has such good sense."

"And pluck to beat the band!" cried Walter. "I'd like to see that country she comes from."

"And me, too," agreed Bess Harley, who overheard this statement.

"'Rose Ranch,'" murmured Grace. "Such a pretty name! After all, she has said just enough about it to be very tantalizing," and the smaller girl smiled.

"Maybe she does that purposely," Bess remarked. "Perhaps she thinks we have so many things she hasn't obtained yet, that she wants to make us jealous a bit."

"I really don't think that Rhoda worries about what she doesn't have," Nan put in. "Perhaps she doesn't even see that she lacks anything that we have."

"Well, she never will go in for athletics," Bess declared.

"Athletics!" burst out Walter. "Why, there isn't another girl at Lakeview Hall who could do what she did just now."

They were all agreed on that point. Even Dr. Prescott and the staff of instructors commented upon Rhoda's stopping the runaway.

Professor Krenner, the mathematics teacher, and with whom Nan and Amelia Boggs took architectural drawing, selected Rhoda to be one of a small party at his cabin up the lake one spring afternoon. And the professor's parties were famous and very much enjoyed by those girls who understood the queer and humorous old gentleman.

He played his key-bugle for them, showed them how to bark birches for the purpose of making canoes (he was building one for his own use) and finally gave them a supper of wild duck, served on birch-bark platters, and corn pone baked on a plank before the embers of a campfire and seasoned mildly with wood smoke.

This incident cheered Rhoda up. She had begun to be dreadfully homesick as the good weather came. She confessed to Nan that she was very much tempted to run away from school and return to the ranch. Only she knew her father and mother would be terribly disappointed in her if she did such a thing.

"And besides that," Rhoda said, with a quiet little smile, "I want company when I go back to Rose Ranch."

"Oh, yes," said the innocent Nan. "You do know people in Chicago, don't you?"

"Humph! Mamma's friend, Mrs. Janeway. Yes," said Rhoda, still secretly amused, "I don't want to go away out to Rose Ranch alone and come back alone next fall. For I've got to come back, I suppose."

"Why, Rhoda!" exclaimed Nan, "I can't see why you don't like Lakeview Hall."

"Wait till you see Rose Ranch. Then you'll know."

"But I don't expect ever to see that," sighed Nan; for she really had begun to think so much about Rhoda's home, and had listened so closely to the tales the Western girl related, that Nan felt herself drawn strongly toward an outdoor experience such as Rhoda enjoyed at home. It would be even more free and primitive, Nan thought, than her sojourn at Pine Camp.

"You are terribly pessimistic," laughed the Western girl in rejoinder to Nan's last observation. "How do you know you'll never see Rose Ranch?"

Even this remark did not make Nan suspect what was coming. Nor did Bess Harley or the Masons have any warning of the plan Rhoda Hammond had so carefully thought out. But the surprise "broke" one afternoon at mail time.

Both Nan and Bess received letters from home, and they ran at once to Room Seven, Corridor Four, to read them. Scarcely had they broken the seals of the two fat missives when the door was flung open and Grace Mason fairly catapulted herself into the room in such a state of excitement that she startled the Tillbury chums.

"What is the matter, Grace?" gasped Bess, as the smaller girl threw herself into Nan's arms.

"Why! she's only happy," said Nan, holding her off and viewing her flushed and animated countenance. "Do get your breath, Gracie."

"And—when I do—I'll take yours!" gasped Grace. She held up a letter. "From mother. She—she says we can go—Walter and I—both of us!"

"Well, for mercy's sake!" exclaimed Bess, "where are you going? Though I should say *you*, Grace, had already gone. Crazy, you know."

"To Rose Ranch!" almost shouted Grace.

In astounded repetition, Nan and Bess fairly shrieked: "*To Rose Ranch?*"

"My goodness, yes! Haven't you heard about it? My letter says Rhoda's invited both of you girls, too, and that Walter is going. Is—it a hoax?"

Nan and Bess stared at each other in amazement for a single moment; then, like a flash, they tore open their own letters, both being those prized "mother letters" so dear to every boarding-school girl's heart, and unfolded the missives the envelopes contained. It was Bess who found it first.

"It's here! It's here! Just think of Rhoda Hammond keeping this secret from us! She wrote her folks and they wrote to mine—and to yours, Nan—and Gracie's. Oh! Oh! We're going, going, going!"

"Isn't it fine?" cried Grace, dancing up and down in her delight.

"Delightsome! Just delightsome!" agreed Bess, coining a new word to express her own joy. "Three cheers and a tiger! And a wildcat! And a panther! And—and—Well! all the other trimmings that may go with three cheers," she concluded because she was out of both breath and inspiration.

"And Rhoda's folks must be awfully nice people," Grace said warmly. "And her mamma—"

But Nan was deep in her own letter from Momsey, and here follows the part of it dealing with this wonderful news which had so excited all three of the girls:

"Your new friend, Rhoda, must be a very lovely girl, and I want you to bring her home to Tillbury the day school closes. I know she must be a nice girl by the way her mother writes me. Her mother is blind, but she has had somebody write me that she wants very much to 'see' Nan Sherwood, who has been so kind to her Rhoda during the latter's first term at Lakeview.

"This makes me very happy and proud, Nan dear; for if your schoolmates love you so much that they write home about you, I am sure you are doing as well at school as Papa Sherwood and I could wish you to. And this Mrs. Hammond is very insistent that you shall visit Rose Ranch this summer. Mrs. Harley came to see me about it, and we have decided that you and Elizabeth can go home with Rhoda, if the Masons likewise agree to let Grace and Walter go. There is a lady going West to Rose Ranch at the same time—a Mrs. Janeway—who is a friend of Mrs. Hammond's. She will look after you young folk en route, and will return with you.

"But we must have you a little while first, my Nan; and you must bring Rhoda here to the little cottage in amity for a few days, at least, before the party starts West. And—"

But this much of the letter was all Nan would let the other girls hear. She was quite as happy as either Grace or Bess. And all three of them tripped away at once to find Rhoda and try to tell her just how delighted they were over this plan.

"It never seemed as though *I* should see Rose Ranch," Nan sighed ecstatically when they had talked it all over. "It is too good to be true."

As the term lengthened the girls were pushed harder and harder by the instructors, and Bess and others like her complained a good deal.

"The only thing that keeps me going is a mirage of Rose Ranch ahead of me," declared Nan's chum, shaking her head over the text books piled upon their study table. "Oh, dear me, Nan! if anything should happen to make it impossible for us to go with Rhoda, I certainly should fall—down—and—die!"

"Oh, nothing will happen as bad as that," laughed Nan.

"Well, nothing much ever does happen to us," agreed Bess. "But suppose something should happen to Rhoda?"

"Shall we set a bodyguard about her?" asked Nan, her eyes twinkling. "Do you think of any particular danger she may be in? I fancy she is quite capable of taking care of herself."

"Now, Nan!" cried Bess, "don't poke fun. It would be awful if anything should happen so that we couldn't go to Rose Ranch with her."

Perhaps this was rather a selfish thought on Bess Harley's part. Still, Bess was not notably unselfish, although she had improved a good deal during the months she had been at Lakeview Hall.

But Nan had occasion to remember her chum's words very clearly not long thereafter, for she did find Rhoda Hammond in trouble. It was one Friday afternoon when Nan was returning from her architectural drawing lesson at Professor Krenner's cabin, up the lake shore. Amelia had not gone that day, being otherwise engaged; so Nan was alone on the path through the spruce wood that here clothed the face of the high bluff on which Lakeview Hall was set.

A company of jays squalling in a thicket had been the only disturbing sounds in the sun-bathed woods, when of a sudden Nan heard somebody speak—a high and angry voice. Then in Rhoda's deeper tones, she heard:

"What do you mean, confronting me like this? I do not know you. You are crazy!"

"Maybe I am cr-r-razy!" cried the second voice, its owner rolling her "r's" magnificently. "But I am not a thief. You, Senorita Ham-mon', are that! You and all your fam-i-lee are the thiefs—yes!"

Nan's thought flashed instantly to the Mexican girl in the shop in Adminster. She had spoken in just this way. And she had given at that time every indication of hating Rhoda.

The girl from Tillbury pushed into the thicket from which the voices sounded. Rhoda replied to the castigation of the other's tongue only by an ejaculation of amazement. The harsher voice went on:

"The tr-r-reasure of the Ranchio Rose—that ees what you have stolen. You and your fam-i-lee. Those reeches pay for your dress—for your ring there on your han'—for all your good times, and to make you a la-dee. But *me*—I am poor that you and yours may be reech, Senorita Ham-mon'. The treasure of the Ranchio Rose belong to me and to my modder—not to you. Thiefs, I say!"

Nan burst through the bushes at this juncture. Rhoda had uttered another cry. She was backing away from a girl with flushed countenance and uplifted, clenched hand—a girl that Nan Sherwood very well remembered.

CHAPTER XI

JUANITA

"STOP that! Don't you dare strike her!" cried Nan, and rushed forward bravely to the rescue of Rhoda Hammond.

Rhoda was bigger and stronger than Nan; but the latter lacked no courage, and she believed that her friend was so much surprised and taken aback by the Mexican girl's accusation that she was not entirely ready to meet the personal assault which the stranger evidently intended.

"Stop that!" repeated Nan, and she dashed between the two girls. She laid her hand upon the Mexican's chest and pushed her back. "You have no right to do this. Don't you know we can have you arrested by the police?"

"Ha! eet ees the odder Senorita," gasped the Mexican girl. "By gracious! I see you are fr-r-riends—heh? You know about the tr-r-reas-ure of the Ranchio Rose—heh?"

"Why, she doesn't know any more what you are talking about than I do," replied Rhoda Hammond, in wonder.

"This girl," said Nan, "must mean the gold and silver and other things you said, Rhoda, that the Mexican bandit hid on your father's ranch somewhere."

"Lobarto!" murmured Rhoda.

"Dhat ees eet!" cried the Mexican girl. "Lobarto, dhe r-r-robber. Lobarto, dhe slayer of women and chil'ren! Ah! The fiend!" and the excited girl's eyes blazed again.

"But what has that to do with Rhoda and her father? I am sure you know very well that Mr. Hammond could not help that bad Mexican bandit's coming up into the vicinity of Rose Ranch and hiding his plunder," said Nan confidently. "And what has it all to do with you, anyway?"

"She!" exclaimed the Mexican girl, pointing to Rhoda. "She ees reech because I am poor. Oh, yes! I know."

"You don't know anything of the kind," said Nan flatly. "Does she, Rhoda?"

"I—I don't know what she means," stammered the girl from Rose Ranch.

"I guess I understand something about it," said the quicker-witted Nan. "She has been robbed by Lobarto, and she thinks your father has found the hidden treasure—the plunder Lobarto left behind at Rose Ranch when he was driven off six years ago."

"You know!" exclaimed the Mexican girl confidently. "How you know?"

"I know what you think. But that doesn't make it so," returned Nan promptly.

"I am sure she is not right in her mind," Rhoda sighed. "What could she have to do with all that treasure they say Lobarto stole in Mexico and hid on our ranch?"

"Come over here and sit down—both of you," commanded Nan, seeing that she had got the Mexican girl quieted for the time being. There was a log in the shade, and they took seats upon it. Nan said kindly to the Mexican: "Now, please, tell us quietly and calmly what you mean."

"Dhat Senorita Ham-mon'—"

"No, no! Begin at the beginning. Don't accuse Rhoda any more. Let us hear all about how you came to know about the treasure, and why you think it is yours."

"Dhat I tell you soon," said the girl quickly. "My modder an' me—"

"Who are you? What is your name?" asked Nan.

"Juanita O'Harra."

"Why! that's both Mexican and Irish," gasped Nan.

"My fader a gre't, big Irisher-man—yes!" said Juanita. "He marry my modder in Honoragas. She have fine hacienda from her papa—yes. She—"

But to put it in more understandable English, as Nan and Rhoda did later when they talked it over with Bess and Grace Mason, Juanita O'Harra told a very interesting—indeed, quite an exciting—story about Lobarto and the lost treasure the bandit chief had carried into the Rose Ranch region.

Juanita's mother had married the Irish contractor who had died when the girl was small. Six years and more before she told this tale to the interested Nan and Rhoda, Lobarto became a scourge of the country about Honoragas. He attacked haciendas, stealing and burning, even maltreating the helpless women and children after killing their defenders.

After robbing the churches, he took all the wealth he had gathered and, with the Mexican Federal troops on his trail, ran up into the United States. How he came to grief there and had to run again with United States troops and the Rose Ranch cowboys behind him, Rhoda had already told her friends.

But that Lobarto had left all the wealth he had stolen somewhere near Rose Ranch, the Mexicans knew as well as the Americans. When captured, members of Lobarto's gang had confessed. But they had been put to death by the Mexican authorities without telling just where the great cache of plunder was.

Juanita and her mother believed that the American owner of Rose Ranch had recovered the treasure and held their share from them. These Mexican people were both ignorant and suspicious. Juanita was very bitter against the *Americanos*, anyway. She had only come up into the States to work so as to support her mother, who remained still on the ruined plantation in Honoragas.

"I went to dhe Ranchio Rose," said Juanita, "and see thees senorita wit' her fader, dhe gre't Senyor Ham-mon'. He laugh at me—yes! He tell me he haf not found dhe tr-r-reasure. But I know better—"

"You do not know anything of the kind," Nan said promptly. "You just have a bad temper and want to hate somebody. Rhoda tells you that she knows nothing about the money and jewels your mother lost. If they are ever found you and your mother shall have them."

"Of course," Rhoda added, "we would not want anything that was not strictly ours. No matter what the law might say about 'findings, keepings,' my father is not that kind, I'd have you know. We haven't found the treasure. If we ever do, I promise you we'll write to your mother at once."

"My modder cannot read the language you speak," said Juanita, sullenly.

"We will have the letter written in Spanish," promised Rhoda.

"Write it to me," said the Mexican girl eagerly. "I must do all business for my modder. Yes. She do not know. She ees ver' poor. But if what Lobarto stole from us is r-recover-red, we shall be reech again. By goodness, yes!"

"In the end," Nan explained to Bess and Grace afterward, "I think we more than half convinced that Mexican girl that it was not her mother's money that dressed Rhoda so nicely."

"How you talk!" exclaimed Rhoda. "I am sorry for that Mex. But, goodness! how mad she was. Just as mad as a lion!"

"'Lion'!" sniffed Bess. "What do you know about lions?"

"We have them about Rose Ranch," said Rhoda, smiling wickedly.

"Oh, never!" squealed Grace.

"Why, lions grow in Africa," said Bess, doubtfully.

"More properly they are pumas, I suppose. But the boys call 'em lions," laughed Rhoda. "Oh, there are a lot of things about Rose Ranch that will surprise you."

"Don't say a word! I guess that is so. Something besides the roses," murmured Bess.

"I shall be afraid to go out of sight of the house," complained Grace, who was timid in any environment. "Don't tell me anything more, Rhoda."

Nevertheless they were all—and all the time—thinking of the trip West. It did not interfere with their standing in classes, but outside of study hours and the time they spent in sleep, the three girls who had been invited by Rhoda to visit Rose Ranch talked of little else. And, of course, Rhoda herself was always willing to talk of her home down near the Mexican Border.

"I am just as sorry for that Mexican girl and her mother as I can be," Rhoda said on one occasion. "I've written daddy about it. I expect he doesn't remember Mrs. O'Harra's coming to Rose Ranch with her daughter about the treasure. You know, that old treasure has made us a lot of trouble."

"I suppose people keep coming up from Mexico looking for it?" suggested Grace.

"Most of them think we have benefited by Lobarto's stealings," sighed Rhoda. "You see, there is much hard feeling on the side of the Mexicans against the Americans. Even the Mexicans born on our side of the Border are not really Americans. They never learn to speak much English, and it makes them clannish and suspicious of English speaking people."

"And how fierce they are!" murmured Nan.

"Juanita would have struck you. Scratched your face, maybe."

"Well, that is only their excitable way. Perhaps she did not really intend to strike me," Rhoda said. "I do wish we could help her and her mother. Somehow, I am sorry for the poor thing."

"Let's get up a searching party when we get to Rose Ranch," said Bess excitedly, "and find that old treasure."

"Wouldn't that be great!" Nan agreed. "But I am afraid if after six years all that plunder hasn't been found, we shouldn't be likely to find it."

"Oh, it's been searched for," Rhoda assured them. "Time and time again. There have been as many men who believed they could find it as ever hunted for the old Pegleg Mine—and that is famous."

"Never say die!" said Bess, nodding her curly head. "I'm going to hunt for it myself."

This raised a laugh; yet every member of the little party, including Walter when he heard the particulars about Juanita, was eagerly interested in the mystery of the treasure of Rose Ranch.

CHAPTER XII

ROSE RANCH AT LAST

The closing of school came at length. Bess had said frankly that she feared it never would come, the time seemed to pass so slowly; but Nan only laughed at her.

"Do you think something has happened to the 'wheels of Time' we read about in class the other day?" she asked her chum.

"Well, it does seem," said merry Bess, "as though somebody must have stuck a stick in the cogs of those wheels, and stopped 'em!"

Both Tillbury girls stood well in their classes; and they were liked by all the instructors—even by Professor Krenner, who some of the girls declared wickedly was the school's "self-starter, Lakeview Hall being altogether too modern to have a crank."

In association with their fellow pupils, Nan and Bess had never any real difficulty, save with Linda Riggs and her clique. But this term Linda had not behaved as she had during the fall and winter semester. This change was partly because of her chum, Cora Courtney. Cora would not shut herself away from the other girls just to please Linda.

Linda had even begun to try to cultivate the acquaintance of Rhoda Hammond—especially when she had heard more about Rose Ranch. But Rhoda refused to yield to the blandishments of the railroad magnate's daughter.

"I suppose it might be good fun to take a trip across the continent to your part of the country," Linda said to the Western girl on one occasion. "You get up such a party, Rhoda, and I'll tease father for his private car, and we will go across in style."

"Thank you," said Rhoda simply. "I prefer to pay my own way."

"No use for Linda to try to 'horn in'—isn't that the Westernism—to our crowd," laughed Bess, when she heard of this. "The 'Riggs Disease' is not going to afflict us this summer, I should hope!"

Cora Courtney, too, had tried to cultivate an acquaintance with Rhoda. But the girl from Rose Ranch made friends slowly. Too many of the girls had ignored her when she first came to Lakeview Hall for Rhoda easily to forget, if she did forgive.

The good-bys on the broad veranda of Lakeview Hall were far more lingering than they had been at Christmas time. The girls were separating for nearly three months—and they scattered like sparks from a bonfire, in all directions.

A goodly company started with the Tillbury chums from the Freeling station; but at each junction there were further separations until, when the time came for the porter to make up the berths, there were only Nan, Bess and Rhoda of all their crowd in the Pullman car. Even Grace and Walter had changed for a more direct route to Chicago.

They awoke in the morning to find their coach sidetracked at Tillbury and everybody hurrying to get into the washrooms. Nan could scarcely wait to tidy herself and properly dress, for there was Papa Sherwood in a great, new, beautiful touring car—one of those, in fact, that he kept for demonstration purposes.

Nan dragged Rhoda with her, while Bess ran merrily to meet what she called "a whole nest of Harley larks" in another car on the other side of the station. It had been determined that Rhoda should go home with Nan.

"Here she is, Papa Sherwood!" cried Nan, leaping into the front of the big car to "get a strangle hold" around her father's neck. "This is our girl from Rose Ranch, Rhoda Hammond. Isn't she nice?"

"I—I can't see her, Nan," said her father. "Whew! let me get my breath and my eyesight back."

Then he welcomed Rhoda, and both girls got into the tonneau to ride to the Sherwood cottage. "Such richness!" Nan sighed.

The little cottage in amity looked just as cozy and homelike as ever. Nothing had been changed there save that the house had been newly painted. As the car came to a halt, the front door opened with a bang and a tiny figure shot out of it, down the walk, and through the gateway to meet Nan Sherwood as she stepped down from the automobile.

"My Nan! My Nan!" shrieked Inez, and the half wild little creature flung herself into the bigger girl's arms. "Come in and see how nice I've kept your mamma. I've learned to brush her hair just as you used to brush it. I'm going to be every bit like you when I get big. Come on in!"

With this sort of welcome Nan Sherwood could scarcely do less than enjoy herself during the week they remained in Tillbury. Inez, the waif, had become Inez, the home-body. She was the dearest little maid, so Momsey said, that ever was. And how happy she appeared to be!

Her old worry of mind about the possibility of "three square meals" a day and somebody who did not beat her too much, seemed to have been forgotten by little Inez. The kindly oversight of Mrs. Sherwood was making a loving, well-bred little girl of the odd creature whom Nan and Bess had first met selling flowers on the wintry streets of Chicago. Of course, during that week at home, the three girls from Lakeview Hall did not sit down and fold their hands. No, indeed! Bess Harley gave a big party at her house; and there were automobile rides, and boating parties, and a picnic. It was a very busy time.

"We scarcely know whether we have had you with us or not, Nan dear," said her mother. "But I suppose Rhoda wants to get home and see her folks, too; so we must not delay your journey. When you come back, however, mother wants her daughter to herself for a little while. We have been separated so much that I am not sure the fairies have not sent a changeling to me!" and she laughed.

At that, for it was not a hearty laugh and Momsey's eyes glistened, if Nan had not given her promise, "black and blue," to Rhoda, she would have excused herself and not gone to Rose Ranch at all. She knew that Momsey was lonely.

But Mrs. Sherwood did not mean to spoil her daughter's enjoyment. And the opportunity to see this distant part of the country was too good to be neglected. Nan might never again have such a chance to go West.

So the three girls were sent off without any tears for the rendezvous with the Masons and Mrs. Janeway at Chicago.

They found Grace and Walter all right; but as the Masons had no idea what Mrs. Janeway looked like, and that lady had no description of the Masons, they had not met. Rhoda had to look up her mother's friend.

"What are you going to do, Rhoda?" asked the bubbling Bess. "Track her down as you would an Indian? Look for signs—?"

"I don't believe in signs," responded Rhoda. "I am going to look for the best dressed woman in Chicago. Such lovely clothes as she wears!"

"I guess that must be so," said Grace as Rhoda walked out of earshot, "for Mrs. Janeway chose Rhoda's own outfit, and you know there wasn't a better dressed girl at Lakeview."

"Wow!" murmured her brother. "What a long tale about dress! Don't you girls ever think of anything but what you put on?"

"Oh, yes, sir," declared Bess smartly. "And you know that Rhoda thinks less about what she wears than most. It's lucky her mother had somebody she could trust to dress her daughter before she appeared at the Hall."

"All on the surface! All on the surface!" grumbled Walter.

"Goodness, Walter," said his sister, "would you want us to swallow our dresses? Of course they are on the surface."

"It certainly is a fact," grinned Walter impudently, "that the curriculum of Lakeview Hall makes its pupils wondrous sharp. Hullo! here comes Rhoda towing a very nice looking lady, I must admit."

In fact, at first sight the three other girls fell in love with Mrs. Janeway. She was a childless and wealthy widow, who, as she asserted, "just doted on girls." She met them all warmly.

"I hope," said Walter, with gravity, as she shook hands with him, "that a mere boy may find favor in your eyes, too. Really, we're not all savages. Some of us are more or less civilized."

"Well," Mrs. Janeway sighed, but with twinkling eyes, "I shall see how well you behave. Now, for our tickets."

"I have the reservations," Walter said quietly. "A stateroom for you four ladies and a berth for me in the same car. In half an hour we pull out. And, girls!"

"Say it," returned Bess.

"Is it something nice, Walter?" asked his sister.

"There is an observation platform on our car—the end car on the train. It goes all the way through to Osaka, where we are going. I think we are fixed just right."

This proved to be the case. The young people pretty nearly lived on that rear platform, for the weather remained pleasant all through the journey. Mrs. Janeway sometimes found it hard work to get them in to go to bed.

The route this tourist car took was rather roundabout; but as Walter said, it landed them at the Osaka station, the nearest railroad point to Rose Ranch, in something like five days.

By this time they were getting a little weary of traveling by rail. Walter declared he was "saddle-sore" from sitting so much. When long lines of corrals and cattle-pens came in sight, Rhoda told them they were nearing Osaka.

"Why, there are miles and miles of those corrals!" cried Bess, in wonder. "You don't mean to say they are all for your father's cattle?"

"Oh, no, my dear. Several ranchers ship from Osaka," explained Rhoda. "And as we all ship at about the same season, there must be plenty of pens and cattle-chutes. Hurry, now. Get your things together."

Bess scrabbled her baggage together, as usual leaving a good deal of it for somebody else to bring. This time it was Walter who gathered up her belongings rather than Nan.

"I never do know what I do with things," sighed Bess. "When I start on a journey I have so few; and when I arrive at my destination it does seem as though I am always in possession of much more than my share. Thank you, Walter," she concluded demurely. "I think boys are awfully nice to have around."

"In that case," said Rhoda, leading the way out of the car as the train slowed down, "you are going to have plenty of boys to wait on you when you get to Rose Ranch. Those punchers are just dying for feminine 'scenery.' I know Ike Bemis once said that he often felt like draping a blanket on an old cow and asking her for a dance."

"The idea!" gasped Mrs. Janeway, who was likewise making her first visit to the ranges.

At that moment Rhoda cried:

"There he is! There's Hess with the ponies."

"Hess who?" asked Grace.

"Hess what?" demanded Nan, as the train stopped and the colored porter quickly set his stool at the foot of the car steps.

"Hesitation Kane," explained Rhoda, hurrying ahead. "Come on, folks! Oh, I am glad to get home!"

Bess, who was last, save Walter, to reach the station platform, gave one comprehensive glance around the barren place.

"Well!" she said. "If this is home—"

"'Home was never like this,'" chuckled Walter.

A few board shacks, the station itself unpainted, sagebrush and patches of alkali here and there, and an endless trail leading out across a vista of flat land that seemed horizonless. The train steamed away, having halted but a moment. To all but Rhoda the scene was like something unreal. "My goodness!" murmured Grace, "even the moving pictures didn't show anything like this."

"They say the desert scenes made by some of the movie companies are photographed at Coney Island. And I guess it's true," said Walter.

Rhoda had run across the tracks toward where a two-seated buckboard, drawn by a pair of eager ponies, was standing. Beside it stood two saddle horses, their heads drooping and their reins trailing before them in the dust. The man who drove the ponies wore a huge straw sombrero of Mexican manufacture. When he turned to look at his employer's daughter the others saw a very solemn and sunburned visage.

"Oh, Hess!" cried Rhoda. "How are you? Is mother all right?"

The man stared unblinkingly at her and his facial muscles never moved. He was thin-lipped, and his hawk nose made a high barrier between his eyes. He did not seem unpleasant, only naturally grim. And silent! Well, that word scarcely indicated the character of Mr. Hesitation Kane.

"Come on!" shouted Rhoda, looking back at her friends, and evidently not at all surprised that the driver of the buckboard did not at once reply to her questions. "Mrs. Janeway, and Nan, and Bess, and Gracie—you all crowd into the buckboard. Walter and I are going to ride. Got my duds here, Hess?"

It was lucky Mr. Kane did not have to answer verbally. He thrust forward a bundle. Rhoda seized it and started for the station where there was a room in which she could change her clothes. Before she quite reached the platform the driver spoke his first word:

"Thanky, Miss Rhody. I'm fine."

Rhoda nodded over her shoulder, laughing at the surprise and amusement of her friends, and disappeared. Walter helped the girls and Mrs. Janeway into the odd though comfortable vehicle. In a few moments Rhoda reappeared in a rough costume that even Mrs. Janeway had to admit did not make the Western girl any the less attractive.

The full breeches and long coat and leggings gave her every freedom of action, and she had put on a wide-brimmed hat. Meanwhile Walter had brought forth from one of his bags a pair of leather riding leggings and buckled on small spurs. He had been forewarned of this ride by Rhoda before they left Chicago.

They mounted the two ponies, and the driver of the buckboard lifted his reins. Then he pulled the eager ponies to a stop again and turned toward Rhoda, answering her second question.

"Yes, ma'am, your mother's fine. She's fine," he announced.

"Don't that beat all!" exclaimed Walter, exploding with laughter as he cantered by Rhoda's side. "That is why we call him 'Hesitation,'" Rhoda said.

"Somebody taught him to count more than ten before speaking, didn't they?" commented Walter.

The trail was not wide enough for the pony riders to keep their mounts beside the buckboard; besides, the dust would have smothered Rhoda and Walter. The light breeze carried the dust off the trail, however; so the two riders could keep within shouting distance of the others.

In two hours or a little more they were out of the barren lands completely. Swerving down an arroyo, all green and lush at the bottom, they cantered up into the mouth of a broad gulch, the walls of which later became so steep that it might well be called a canyon.

The ponies never walked—up grade, or down. They cantered or galloped. Hesitation Kane never spoke to them; but they seemed to know just what he wanted them to do by the way he used the reins—and they did it.

"I don't see how he does it," said Walter to Rhoda. "It doesn't seem really possible that one could make a horse understand without speech."

"Oh, he can speak to them if it is necessary. But he says it isn't often necessary to speak to a horse. The less you talk to them the better trained they are. And Hess is daddy's boss wrangler."

"'Wrangler'?"

"Horse wrangler. Horse trainer, that means."

"But, my goodness!" chuckled Walter, "'to wrangle' certainly means quarreling in speech. I should think it was almost like a Quaker meeting when this Mr. Kane trains a pony."

"It is a fact," laughed Rhoda, "that the ponies make much more noise than Hesitation does."

As they entered this deeper gulch, the girls cried out in delight. The trail was narrow and grassy. Growing right up to the path—so that they could stretch out their hands and pick them—were acres and acres of wild roses. They scented the air and charmed the eye for miles and miles along the trail.

They rode on and on. Finally the little cavalcade wound out of the gap, down a slope, crossed a tumbling river that was yards broad but not very deep, and the ponies quickened their pace as they mounted again to a higher plain.

"There it is!" shouted Rhoda, and, waving her hat, she spurred her pony ahead and passed the buckboard at full speed.

On a knoll the others saw a low-roofed, but wide-spreading, bungalow sort of structure, with corrals and sheds beyond. The latter were bare and ugly enough; but the ranch house was almost covered to the eaves with climbing roses in luxurious bloom.

CHAPTER XIII

OPEN SPACES

"On, Nan!" cried Bess, squeezing her chum's arm, "what do you think of it?"

"It is more beautiful than I had any idea of! And Rhoda had to come away from all this just to go to school," answered the equally excited Nan.

Here Grace Mason's usual timidity showed itself, as she said:

"But there is so much of it! We must have come twenty miles from the railroad station."

"More than that," put in her brother, from his seat in the saddle.

"I don't care!" cried Bess. "It's wonderful."

"Oh, it is wonderful, I grant you," said Grace. "But—but everything is so big—and open—and lonesome."

"Cheer up, Sis," said Walter. "We are all here to keep you company, to say nothing of the cows and the horses," and he laughed.

Mrs. Janeway's opinion was practical to say the least, for her first words were, as the buckboard reached the house: "I certainly shall be glad to get a bath."

Rhoda had thrown herself from her pony and rushed up the steps of the veranda to greet two persons who, later, the visitors found were Mr. and Mrs. Hammond. The former was a rather heavily built, shaggy-bearded man, his face burned to a brick-red and such part as the beard did not hide covered with fine lines like a veil. His wife was a tall and graceful woman who showed nothing in her clear, wide-open eyes of her blindness which for so many years had set her apart from other people.

The blind woman stepped with assurance to the edge of the veranda to greet the visitors, and it was Mrs. Janeway she first met and embraced.

"Marian Janeway! How I wish I could see you, to know if you have really changed!" cried Mrs. Hammond in the heartiest and most cheerful voice imaginable. It was easy to see from whom Rhoda had got her voice.

"I've grown fat—I can tell you that," sighed the Chicago woman. "And you—why, you are still as graceful as you were when you were a girl."

"Flatterer!" exclaimed Rhoda's mother, laughing. Then she seized upon Nan who chanced to come up the steps directly behind Mrs. Janeway.

"Who is this?" she cried. "Wait!" Her fingers ran quickly but lightly over Nan's countenance. She even felt her ears, and the hair where it fluffed over her brow, and traced the line of her well marked eyebrows. "Why!" she added with decision, "this is Nan Sherwood that I have heard so much about."

"Oh, Mrs. Hammond," gasped the girl, "how did you know?"

She looked up into the shining face of the blind woman and could scarcely believe that she was so afflicted. Mrs. Hammond's laugh was deep-throated and hearty, like Rhoda's own.

"I know you, my dear, because Rhoda has told me so much about you. She has explained your character, I see, very truthfully. Your features bear out all she has said. You see, my dear, I am a witch!" and she kissed Nan warmly.

She welcomed the others with grace and that wide hospitality which is only found, perhaps, in the West and among people of the great outdoors. It arises from old times, when the wanderer, seeing a campfire, was sure of a welcome if he approached, and a welcome without questioning.

Mr. Hammond was equally glad to see the young folk. He spoke with a pleasant drawl, and aside from his gray hair and beard revealed few marks of age. His vigorous frame carried too much flesh, perhaps; but that was, he said, "because he took it easy and let the boys run things to suit themselves."

This last statement, however, Nan, who was observant, took with the proverbial pinch of salt. The expression of his countenance was kindly, but his character was firm and he spoke at times with a decision that made the servants, for instance, hurry to obey him. He was, indeed, a very forceful man; but Nan Sherwood liked him immensely.

The rambling ranch house covered a deal of ground and was two stories high. The rooms were low-ceilinged, the upper rooms especially so. The girls who had come to visit Rhoda had a big, plainly furnished, airy room on the upper floor, beside Rhoda's own chamber. Walter had his choice of a bed or a hammock in a room across the hall. The adults of the household were disposed below, while the servants occupied quarters away from the main dwelling.

There was a water system which afforded plenty of baths, the clank of the pump being heard in a steady murmur from somewhere behind the house. It was too late, when they were freshened after the ride, for any exploration outside the house on this evening. All the visitors were ready for dinner when the Mexican waiter announced it.

The servants included a Chinese cook, Mexican houseboys, and negroes for the outside work. The life at Rose Ranch was evidently a rather free and easy existence. The standards of etiquette were not just the same as at the Mason house in Chicago; but the Hammonds knew well how to make their guests feel at home. The quality of the hospitality of the ranchman and his wife was not strained.

The party lingered long at dinner, under the glow of a hanging lamp that illuminated the table but left the corners and sides of the great room in shadow. Now and then somebody would lounge in at the doorway and speak to Mr. Hammond.

"Ah say, Boss, where'd you say Dan's outfit was goin'? I plumb forgot."

"You'd forget your head, Carey, if it wasn't screwed on tight," declared the ranchman, without glancing at the big figure slouching in the doorway. "Dan and his bunch light out for Beller's Gulch come mornin'."

A little later it was a lighter step, and the jingle of spurs on the veranda floor.

"Tumbleweed done sprung his knee, Mist' Ham-mon'. Kyan't use him nohow fo' a while."

"My lawsy!" ejaculated Rhoda's father, "seems to me most of you fellers ain't fitted to take care of a saw horse, let alone a sure enough pony. Some of you will have to ride mules if you don't stop ruinin' my horseflesh."

"Wal, Tumbleweed is right fidgety," complained the cowboy.

"What do you want to ride—somethin' broke to a side-saddle?" demanded the ranchman in disgust. "Go rope a new pony out of that band Hesitation's just brought up. And be mighty careful not to get an outlaw. Hess says there's two or three in that band that are fresh out of the hills."

These side remarks excited Walter. The girls, too, were interested. Grace said she hoped there was not any horse as bad as the pony that ran away at Lakeview, and which Rhoda had stopped so dexterously.

"My *dear!*" laughed Rhoda, "that wasn't a bad pony. She was only frisky. But Hess shall find you a perfectly safe mount."

"I hope you will extend that promise to me," said Nan, laughing. "If I am to ride I want something I can stay on."

"No bucking broncos for me, either," cried Bess. "At least, not until I have learned to ride better than I do at present."

They went to bed that night wearied after traveling so far, but much excited as to what the next day would bring forth.

CHAPTER XIV

THE POOR LITTLE CALF

Nan awoke when it was still utterly dark. Nothing had frightened her, and yet she felt that something really important was about to happen—something wonderful! What it could be, she had no idea. Her imagination was not at all spurring her mind. She only knew that she was on the verge of a new and surprising experience.

There were three beds in the big room, and she could hear Bess and Grace breathing calmly in their own cots. But she was wide awake.

Without speaking, or making any more sound than she could help, Nan Sherwood crept out of bed. The air from the open windows was chill, so she knew it must be near dawn.

She slipped her feet into slippers and shrugged her robe about her. Then she crept to the nearest casement. She had to kneel to see out, for the window, which looked to the east, was under the eaves of the ranch house. The sill was only a foot above the floor.

Nan folded her arms on this sill and looked out into the velvety darkness. A great silence seemed to brood over the country which she could not see. She remembered how lonely the ranch house seemed to be when she had first seen it the previous afternoon. Even the bunk houses where the help slept were at some distance, and not in this easterly direction.

Blackness seemed to have shut down all about the great dwelling, like a curtain. The roses weighted the air with their delicious scent. She even had to reach forth and separate the prickly vines carefully so as to make an opening through which she hoped soon to see.

For she knew now what it was that had awakened her—what it was that was about to happen. Dawn was coming! The sun would soon appear! A new day was in the making just below the horizon which she could not see.

A haze had been drawn over the stars; therefore there was absolutely no light in the world. Not yet. But—

There it was! A pale gray streak was drawn along the very edge of the world, far, far away. It was just as though a brushful of gray paint had been dashed along that line where the earth and the sky met.

The gray line remained, though growing more distinct, while above it a band of faint pink rimmed the east as far as she could see. Nan drew her kimono about her shoulders and shivered ecstatically. This was the wonderful thing that she had awakened with in her mind.

Sunrise!

A gun could have shot the earth away out there across the rolling plain no more suddenly with yellow than now was done by the sun's reflection. It had not come into sight yet; but Nan could see the colors reaching upward toward the zenith. A riot of color hurried everywhere, over the earth and up in the sky; and then—

"There he is!" shouted Nan aloud, as the edge of a fiery red ball appeared.

"What is the matter with you, Nan Sherwood?" complained Bess, from her bed.

"Oh, what is it? Nan!" shrieked Grace, sitting straight up in bed and evidently expecting that the very worst had happened.

"It's morning, you lazy things," whispered Nan. "Sh! Get up and see the most wonderful sight you ever did see."

"I bet the sun is getting up in the west," gasped Bess, hopping out of bed at this announcement.

Already there was a stir about the place. Down at the bunk houses the dogs began to yap and some full-throated cow-puncher sent forth a "Yee! Yee! Yee! Yip!" that acted as rising call for all the hands. As the three girls from so much farther east gathered at the low window to peer out, there sounded another cowboy salute and there dashed by with the drumming of hoofs a little party of mounted men who rode just as the cowboys do in the moving pictures.

Rhoda burst into the room and ran to hug her three friends. She was already dressed.

"There goes Dan's bunch already," she said. "And see 'em turn and look back. They're just showing off; they know we sleep on this side of the house. Daddy will give them a wigging, for maybe Mrs. Janeway wants to sleep."

Breakfast was an early repast at Rose Ranch. Mrs. Hammond and Mrs. Janeway were served in their rooms; but the rest of the family were soon at the table. It was a bountiful repast, with Ah Foon, the Chinese cook, coming to the door every few minutes to see for himself if the flapjack plates did not need replenishing.

"We are going to get our ponies first of all," Rhoda announced. "Oh! I am so hungry for a ride—a good ride—again."

"But, goodness! don't we have to be fitted to them?" demanded Bess, the incorrigible. "I would not like to walk right up to a pony and say 'You're mine!'—just like that!"

"Hess will pick them out for us, won't he. Daddy?"

"I reckon so," said her father, without looking up from his mail that one of the Mexicans had brought in the minute before.

"Goodness!" exclaimed Grace. "We'll never be able to get the ponies to-day, then, that is sure. He won't be able to answer you so quickly."

"That's all right," laughed Rhoda. "I asked him about them last night"

They ran out to the corral as soon as the girls got into their new riding habits. They had had them made something like Rhoda's.

"You see," the latter had said, "our ponies are not often trained for side-saddles and skirts. And, then, they are dangerous."

The silent Hesitation was on hand. He had a bunch of ponies gathered in a particular corral, and pointed to them in answer to Rhoda when she asked if they were perfectly safe. About the time the girls and Walter had looked them over and chosen those they liked, the horse wrangler said:

"All broke for tenderfoots. You can trust any of 'em as long as you keep your eyes open."

"Well," murmured Bess, "I certainly do not intend to ride horseback when I am asleep."

Nan chose for herself a cunning little fat pony, with brown and white patches and a pink nose. In the East it would have been called a calico pony; but Rhoda called it a pinto.

The Eastern girls were just a little doubtful of their mounts, because their tails and ears were always twitching and they seemed quite unable to "make their feet behave."

"Mine is just as nervous as I am," confessed Bess, as she gathered up the reins. "If he starts as quick as Walter's does, I know I shall be thrown as high as the cow jumped—over the moon."

"Have no fear, Elizabeth," advised Nan. "Try to copy Rhoda, and you'll stick on all right."

"Oh, I'll be a regular copy-cat," promised her chum. "I don't wish to be carried back to Tillbury in pieces."

The little cavalcade started off from the corrals in good order. They went past the house and waved their hands to Mrs. Janeway and shouted a greeting to Rhoda's mother. Then the ranch girl led them at a fast canter toward the west.

When Walter saw the small rifle tucked into a case under Rhoda's knee he expressed the wish that he had brought his own rifle West.

"Do you know, I never thought of it! You're not expecting to shoot Indians, are you, Rhoda?" he said jokingly.

"You never can tell," she replied, smiling. "But they say I am a pretty good shot. I don't expect to shoot an Indian."

"I can shoot, too," said Grace quickly. "Walter taught me last year."

"Mercy! what did you shoot with, Grace?" demanded Bess. "A squirt-gun?"

"A pistol and Walter's rifle. I know I'm awfully scared of 'em, but I wanted to know which was the more dangerous end of a gun."

"Bravo!" cried Nan, laughing.

"Why, if you want, I can supply you all with firearms," said Rhoda. "There are plenty at the ranch. And the boys most always lug around a 'gat,' as they call 'em, because of the coyotes."

"Oh, dear me! are they dangerous?" demanded Grace.

"The coyotes? Only to stray calves and lame cattle. We seldom see anything more dangerous. And as long as you are on horseback you are perfectly safe, anyway, even from a lion."

"There she goes talking about lions again," murmured Bess. "I feel as though I were on the African veldt."

"Let's all learn how to use firearms," said Nan eagerly. "Why shouldn't we?"

"Why, Nan Sherwood! you have the instincts of a desperado," declared her chum. "I can see that."

"I want to do just as the Western girls do while I am here," said Nan.

"So I, I presume," Rhoda queried, "should wish to do just as the Eastern girls do when I am at Lakeview?"

"Well, you'd get along better," Nan argued, quite seriously.

Out of sight of the ranch house they very quickly found themselves in what seemed to the visitors a pathless plain. Off to the left a huge herd of red and white cattle was feeding. It was broken up into little groups and the creatures looked no more harmful than cows back home. There was not a herdsman in sight.

"Why," said Bess, "I expected to see cowboys riding around and around the cattle all the time, and hear them singing songs."

"They do do that at night. The riding, anyway. And most of the boys try to sing. It takes up time and keeps 'em from being lonely," replied Rhoda. "But I am not sure that the cows are fond of the singing. They are patient creatures, however, and endure a good deal."

"Now, Rhoda!" exclaimed Nan, "don't squash all our beliefs about the cowpunching industry which we have learned from nursery books and movies."

Rhoda headed away from the herd, and by and by they descended a steep but grassy slope into the mouth of a rock-walled canyon. It was a wild-looking place; but there were clumps of roses growing here and there. Rhoda leaped down and let her pony stand, with the reins trailing before him on the ground.

"Isn't he cunning!" observed Bess. "He thinks he's hitched."

"They are trained that way. You see, on the plains there are so few hitching posts," said Rhoda dryly.

The others dismounted, too. Rhoda was hunting among the great boulders that littered the grassy bottom. When they asked her what she was looking for, she called back that she would show them a boiling spring if she could find it.

Suddenly Nan lifted her head to listen. Then she started up the canon, which, in that direction, grew narrower between the walls.

"Don't you hear that calf bawling?" she demanded, when Bess asked her where she was going.

"Oh, I hear it," said Bess, keeping in the rear. "But how do you know it is a calf?"

"Then it is something imitating one very closely," sniffed Nan, and kept on. The next minute she shouted back: "It is! A little, cunning, red calf. And, oh, Bess! it has hurt its leg."

She ran forward. Bess followed with more caution. Suddenly there was a crash in the bushes, and out into the open, right beside the injured calf, came a red and white cow. This animal bawled loudly and charged for a few yards directly toward Nan Sherwood.

"Oh, goodness, Nan! Come away!" begged Bess, turning to run. "That old cow will bite you."

But it was not the anxious mother of the calf that had startled Nan. She knew she could dodge the cow. But above the place where the calf lay, on a great gray rock that gave it a commanding position, the girl saw a huge, cat-like creature with glaring eyes and a switching tail.

She had never seen a puma, not even in a menagerie. But she could not mistake the slate and fawn colored body, the cocked ears, the bristling whiskers, and the distended claws, the latter working just like a cat's when the latter is about to make a charge.

And it looked as though the savage beast could quite overleap the cow and calf and almost reach Nan Sherwood's feet.

CHAPTER XV

A TROPHY FOR ROOM EIGHT

Nan was badly frightened. But she had once faced a lynx up at Pine Camp, and had come off without a scratch. Now she realized that this mountain lion had much less reason for attacking her than had the lynx of the Michigan woods; for the latter had had kittens to defend.

The huge puma on the rock glared at her, flexed his shoulder muscles, and opening his red mouth, spit just like the great cat he was. Really, he was much more interested in the bleating red calf than he was in the girl who was transfixed for the moment in her tracks.

Bess, who could not see the puma, kept calling to Nan to look out for the cow. She was more in fun than anything else, for she did not believe the cow could catch her chum if the latter ran back.

What amazed Bess Harley was the fact that Nan stood so long by the clump of brush which hid the rock on which the puma crouched from Bess's eyes.

"What is the matter with you?" gasped Bess at last "You look like Lot's wife, though you are too sweet ever to turn to salt, my dear. Come on!"

Then, of a sudden, Bess heard the big cat spit! "My goodness!" she shrieked, "what is that?"

Her cry was heard by Rhoda, at a distance. The Western girl knew that something untoward was taking place. She ran for her pony and leaped into the saddle.

"What is it?" she shouted to Bess, whom she could see from horseback.

"Nan's found a red calf—and he makes the queerest noise," declared the amazed Bess. "I'm afraid of that calf."

Walter ran to mount his pony, too. But Rhoda spurred directly toward the spot where Bess stood. Being in the saddle, she was so much higher than Nan's chum that she could see right over the brush clump. Immediately she beheld Nan and the crouching lion.

"Come back, Nan!" she called quickly. "Stoop!"

She snatched the rifle from under her knee. It leaped to her shoulder, and, standing up in her stirrups while her pony stood quivering and snorting, for he had smelled the puma, the girl of Rose Ranch took quick but unerring aim at the crouching, slate-colored body on the boulder.

The beast was about to spring. Indeed, he did leap into the air. But that was the reflex of his muscles after the bullet from Rhoda's rifle struck him.

She had come up so that her sight had been most deadly—right behind the fore shoulder. The ball entered there, split the beast's heart, and came out of his chest. He tumbled to the ground, kicking a bit, but quite dead before he landed.

"There!" exclaimed Rhoda, "I warrant that's the lion daddy was speaking to Steve about last night. He said it wasn't coyotes that killed all the strays. He had seen the tracks of this fellow in the hills."

"Rhoda!" shrieked Bess, "is that a lion?"

"Most certainly, my dear."

"Hold me, somebody! I want to faint," gasped Bess. "And he almost jumped right down our Nan's throat."

"No," said Nan. "Scared as I was, I knew enough to keep my mouth shut."

But none of them were really as careless as they sounded. Rhoda jumped down and hugged Nan. It was true that something might have happened to the latter if the lion had missed his intended prey.

"And we'll have to shoot the poor calf. It's broken its leg," the ranch girl said, after the congratulations were over.

The red and white cow still stood over the calf and bellowed. She would occasionally run to the dead puma and try to toss it; but she did not much like the near approach of human beings, either.

"I tell you what," Walter said, examining the dead puma with a boy's interest: "That was an awfully clean shot, Rhoda. The pelt won't be hurt. You should have this skin cured and made into a rug."

"Oh, yes!" cried Bess. "Take it back to Lake-view Hall with you, Rhoda, and decorate Room Eight, Corridor Four!"

"Come along, then," the Western girl said, smiling. "We'll ride over to the herd and send one of the boys back to skin the lion and butcher the veal, too. We might as well eat that calf as to leave him for the coyotes."

They hurried away from the vicinity of the dead puma, and, to tell the truth, for the rest of the ride the visitors from the East kept very close together.

"To think," sighed Bess, when they had dismounted at the house some time later and given the ponies over to the care of two Mexican boys who came up from the corrals for them, "that one is liable to run across lions and tigers and all kinds of wild beasts so near such a beautiful house as this. It must have been a dream."

"That puma skin doesn't look like a dream," said Walter, laughing and pointing to the pelt of the beast which hung from Rhoda's saddle and made all the ponies nervous.

"Well," said Bess, with determination, "I am willing to learn to shoot. And hereafter I won't go out of our bedroom without strapping a pistol to my waist."

They all laughed at this statement. But they spent that afternoon, with revolvers and light rifles, on what Rhoda called "the rifle range," down behind the bunk houses. Hesitation Kane, the horse wrangler, as silent almost as the sphinx, drifted out to the spot and showed them by gestures, if not by many words, how to hit the bull's-eye. Nan, as well as her chum, became much interested in this sport. The adventure with the big puma really had made Nan feel as though she should know how to use a gun.

Several days passed before the party rode far from Rose Ranch again. But every day the young folks were in the saddle for a few hours, and all became fair horsewomen—all but Walter, of course, who was already a horseman.

There was great fun inside the big ranch house, as well as in the open. In the evenings, especially, the young people's fun drew all the idle hands about the place, as well as the family itself.

There were a player-piano and a fine phonograph in the big drawing-room. The windows of this room opened down to the floor, and the cowboys from the bunk house, the Mexicans, and even Ah Foon, gathered on the side porch to hear the music.

When a dance record was put on the machine the clatter of boots on the piazza betrayed more than one pair of punchers solemnly dancing together.

"Though," complained Rhoda's father, "those spurs the boys wear will be the ruination of my hardwood floor. Where do they think they are? At a regular honky-tonk? None of 'em's got right good sense."

"Let them dance, daddy," said his wife, who usually called the ranch owner by the same pet name his daughter used. "They don't often get a chance up here at the big house to show off. You and I might better be out there, dancing with them."

"My glory, Ladybird!" gasped Mr. Hammond, in mock alarm. "I'm in my stockin' feet. I'd get 'em full of splinters, like enough."

"Then, Walter, you come and dance with me," the blind woman cried. "I'm bound to dance with somebody."

And to see her weaving in and out among the dancers in Walter's grasp, one would never guess her affliction.

That evening's entertainment was only an impromptu affair. A few nights later the house party was formally invited to a "ball" at the men's quarters. The big dining room next the bunk house was cleared out, two fiddles and an accordion obtained from Osaka, and the Rose Ranch outfit showed the visitors what a real cowboy dance was like.

Rhoda and her friends certainly had a fine time at this ball. Boys from neighboring outfits attended, some riding fifty and sixty miles to "shake a leg" as the local expression had it.

There were both Mexican and white girls from Osaka and from other ranches. Even a party of Indians attended, but the young squaws were in civilized costume and looked even more "American" than the Mexican girls. One young Indian, however, confided to Walter that he did not think the new dances were graceful or really worthy.

"Really, the square dances and the good old waltz are more to my taste," he said. "We never took up these one—and two-steps at Carlisle when I was there."

"Another of my cherished beliefs gone," confessed Walter, afterward, to Nan. "I bet that redskin doesn't know how to throw the tomahawk, and that he couldn't give the warhoop the proper pronunciation if he tried. Dear me! this Southwest is getting awfully civilized."

But Bess Harley was delighted with the evening's fun. Going to bed at midnight, she said:

"Dear me, Rhoda, what perfectly lovely times you can have out here in the wilderness. I never danced with so many nice boys before. I never would have believed Rose Ranch was like this."

CHAPTER XVI

EXPECTATIONS

After this Nan and Bess and Grace, as well as Walter, were well acquainted with the "boys" about Rose Ranch. At least, they knew all those employed within easy riding distance of the ranch house.

It was later that they learned they had met none of "Dan's bunch." That was the crowd that had ridden away the very morning after the visitors had arrived at the ranch. The outfit headed by Dan MacCormack had gone to round up a horse herd many miles from headquarters.

Mr. Hammond and several other ranchmen of the vicinity allowed their horses to run wild in the hills for a part of each year. The larger part, in fact.

"You see, they get their own living up there, on pasturage that they never could be driven to," Rhoda explained to the girls. "Besides, many of the finest mustangs in the country run wild and will never be caught. Daddy likes to have his herds crossed with that wild blood. It makes the colts more vigorous and handsomer. Oh, I just wish you girls could see some of the wild stallions. But they seldom come down with the herds to the rodeo. They go back into the wilder hills with the scrubs that the boys don't care to drive in.

"About this time of year the several bands belonging to Rose Ranch and our neighbors are driven down to the lowlands. The mares and yearlings are already branded, of course; so the various owners cut out their own animals, and the young colts, of course, run with their mothers.

"Each ranch outfit knows its own colts and brands accordingly. We call it a round-up. 'Rodeo' is Mexican for it. We drive them into the branding pens and mark the colts. Then we cut out the horses that are needed on the ranch, or to train for sale, and let the others drift again."

"And do all the poor horses have to be burned?" murmured Grace, with a shudder.

"And our cattle, too. How else would we know them from other people's cattle?" demanded Rhoda. "It's nowhere near so horrid as it sounds. The smart is soon over. And, really, how else could we tell the creatures apart?"

"Goodness! don't ask *me*" said Grace. "I am not in the cattle business."

But she confessed to Nan that she intended to shut her eyes tight when the poor little colts were to be burned, and stuff her fingers into her ears, too. However, she and the other girls were very eager to attend the round-up; and a messenger from Dan, the sub-foreman, had come in to headquarters with the announcement that the herdsmen from the combined ranches were driving down the biggest bunch of horses in a decade.

"You and your party, Rhoda, can start away in the morning, bright and early," said her father at dinner that night. "I've sent away a grub wagon and Ah Foon's right bower to cook for you. I know you'd cause a famine if you depended on the regular chuck wagon of Dan's outfit. There isn't but one sleeping tent; Walter will have to rough it."

"That will not bother me, Mr. Hammond," declared the boy. "I've camped out more than once."

"'Twon't be much of a punishment to sleep out-of-doors this weather," said the old ranchman. "All that may bother you is a tornado. We have 'em occasionally at this season."

"And what do you do when there is a tornado, Mr. Hammond?" asked Bess, interested.

"Only one thing to do—hold tight and keep your hair on," chuckled Mr. Hammond. "If you really do get in the path of one, lie down and cling to the grass-roots till it blows over."

"Oh! A cyclone!" cried Bess.

"Not exactly. A cyclone, I reckon, is some worse. A cyclone is a twister. They say if a cyclone hits a pig end to, and the wrong way, it twists his tail to the left instead of to the right and he's never the same pig again."

"Now, daddy!" complained Rhoda, "what do you want to tell such awful jokes for? Nothing like that ever happened to our pigs."

"Well," said her father, his eyes twinkling, "we never had a real cyclone down here. But tornadoes are bad enough."

It was barely daybreak the next morning when the sleepy peons brought the ponies to the house. Rhoda knew the trail well, and within the precincts of Rose Ranch, at least, her father did not consider it necessary for any guard to ride with her.

"I often ride to Osaka for the mail," explained Rhoda. "What should I be afraid of?"

"Aren't there any tramps?" murmured Grace.

"Well," laughed Rhoda, "not the kind you mean. Tramps afoot would not get far in this country. And how could a man on foot catch me? Your kind of tramps don't go far from the railroad lines. And if there are any other ne'er-do-wells in the neighborhood, they know daddy too well to molest me. You see, daddy used to be sheriff in the old days. And he has a reputation," laughed Rhoda.

This conversation occurred just after they left the house on this windy morning, with a red sun coming up behind them "as big as a cartwheel," Bess announced. The level rays of the sun shot far, far across the plains and gilded the line of buttes and mesas Rhoda had told them so much about while back at Lakeview Hall.

"Those are not the Blue Buttes this morning, Rhoda," declared Nan. "They are golden."

Rhoda's eyes swept the frontage of the eminences. She carried a pair of glasses in a case slung from her shoulder. Suddenly she seized these, uncased them, and clapped them to her eyes.

"Hi, cap'n!" cried Bess, "what do you spy?"

"See that flash between those two hills?" said Rhoda, reining in her mount.

They gathered about her, looking where she aimed the glasses. Walter exclaimed:

"I see the flash! It isn't the sun shining on guns, is it?"

"Nonsense!" cried Nan Sherwood.

"No-o," said Rhoda. "People don't carry guns that way around here. Besides, the only part of a gun that the sun would flash on would be the bayonet; and we don't carry army rifles in this country," and she laughed.

"There it is again!" exclaimed Walter.

"I see it, too," said Nan. "Rhoda, what can it be? Something is surely moving this way on a road."

"That is the old Spanish Trail," said the Rose Ranch girl. "It is the trail I told you about, by which the old *Conquistadors* of Cortez reached this part of the country. And it is the most direct road into Mexico."

"It must be some kind of caravan coming through there," said Bess dryly.

"You are quite right," Rhoda declared. "A party of horsemen are riding this way. And they are Mexicans."

"Rhoda!" cried Nan, "you can't see that through those glasses."

"No; I cannot distinguish the horsemen. But I can see the little flashes moving across the saddle of the Gap and down into the valley on this side. And I know they are Mexicans because those flashes are the sun's rays shining on the silver trimming on their sombreros. Yes, they are Mexicans."

"Glory be!" exclaimed Bess. "Can you be sure of all that?"

"More. Poor Mexicans—the peons who come up here to find work—do not wear such sombreros. Nor do many Mexicans waste their money in such fashions nowadays. But there is a class that dress just that fancily."

"Who are they?"

"Men that the ranchers here will not want to see. I know that daddy will ride over to the rodeo behind us, or I would turn about now and run to tell him. There! they are gone. There must have been a dozen of them."

"But who are they?" demanded Nan, anxiously.

"Of course, I am not positive. But I think," said Rhoda, closing the glasses and putting them in the case again, "that they are a band of wanderers. Perhaps a raiding party led by one of the so-called 'liberators' of Mexico. You know, there are more 'liberators' in Mexico than you can shake a stick at," and the girl of Rose Ranch laughed.

"You mean bandits!" cried Nan.

"Well, that is a harsh word. They are political leaders for the most part. Sometimes they become important leaders. But when they come over on this side of the Border they need just as close watching as a pack of wolves."

"Are these men like that Lobarto you told us about?" said Walter.

"Perhaps. Of course, I do not really know. Let us ride along, and when daddy overtakes us, I will tell him."

CHAPTER XVII

THE ROUND-UP

Mr. Hammond, however, did not overtake the young people before they reached the mouth of the canyon through which Rhoda said the army of horses must be driven down to the branding pens.

"Of course, we could go on to the pens and wait there," she said to her friends. "Our personal outfit is there already. Daddy sent it over last night But then you would miss a sight that I want you all to take back East with you as a memory. It is something you will never forget."

"Go on, Rhoda," said Bess. "Show us. Of course, we haven't been seeing wonderful things right along ever since we arrived at Rose Ranch!"

"This is something special," said Rhoda, and led the way into the canyon at a quick canter.

The high-walled slash in the foothills narrowed rapidly, and five miles from the mouth of it the walls were so close together that Walter declared he could throw a stone from one to the other.

The way was becoming rocky, too; the patches of grass were meager and the brush grew more sparse.

The summit of the bare walls rose higher and higher. Far above the cut a vulture wheeled. The sun beat down into the canon, for it was now mid-forenoon, and, the breeze having died, the party of riders began to suffer from the heat.

"I'm melting," declared Bess. "But that's a small matter. I was getting too fat, anyway."

"Listen!" commanded Rhoda suddenly.

They heard then a growing sound like the rolling of many barrels at a distance. It was not thunder. The sky was as clear as a bell.

"Quick!" exclaimed Rhoda. "We must get up yonder in that cleft! See? And keep a tight rein on your ponies."

They rode quickly off the trail, while the strange sound grew in volume. It certainly was something coming down the canyon; but the huge boulders shut out all view of what lay thirty yards away from the party.

They reached a small cleared space against the foot of one cliff, but some yards above the bottom of the canyon. Now, as the growing sound came nearer, Nan shouted:

"I know what it is! It's the herd of horses."

Rhoda nodded. The clatter of the countless hoofs came nearer and nearer. The girls and Walter dismounted, and Rhoda warned them to stand in front of their mounts and keep the bridle-reins in their hands.

They could not yet see the head of the herd; but above the boulders they saw a cloud of dust rising. This dust rolled down the canyon and reached the observers first. Then appeared several horsemen riding at a sharp canter. The range horse almost never trots.

Rhoda had to shout to make her voice heard by her friends above the clatter of hoofs:

"Some of those are our men; others belong to the Long Bow, Gridiron, and Bar One outfits. They are leading the herd and will spread out at the mouth of the canyon and keep the flanks of the mob from drifting."

"Oh! The ponies!" shrieked Bess suddenly.

Out of the rolling dust cloud below them were thrust the bobbing heads, shaking manes, and plunging forefeet of the leaders of the herd. Black horses, red horses, gray, white, all shades of roan, pinto, and the coveted buckskin color, which always sells well in the West.

The tossing manes became like the surf of an angry sea. The thunder of hoofs was all but deafening. Above this noise sounded the shrill whistling of the male horses and the answering neighs of the half-mad herd.

There was reason for clinging to the bridles of the saddled ponies from Rose Ranch. They began to answer the cries of the wild mob below, and stamped their little hoofs upon the rock. Bess Harley's mount stood up on his hind legs, and if Walter had not caught the reins the brute might have got away.

"Why, you naughty boy!" cried Bess. "I never would have thought you'd do it. He seemed so tame, Rhoda!"

Rhoda could not hear her, but shook a warning head. While the herd was passing one could not trust even the best trained saddle pony. It was only a few months before that they had all been members of just such a mob of wild horses as this.

The dust was carried to the other side of the canyon by such air as was stirring; therefore Rhoda and her visitors obtained a better view of the horses as the herd flowed on. There seemed to be an endless stream of them. Hundreds—yes, thousands—plunged down the canon trail, sure footed as sheep over the rocky path.

The girls fairly squealed with delight when they saw the long-legged colts staggering along close to their mothers' flanks. There was no play among them, for without doubt the younger creatures were all much confused, and very tired.

Had there been any place where the mates could have turned out of the mob with their young, they would undoubtedly have done so; but the way was narrow and those behind pushed the others on. After all, Nan secretly thought, it was a cruel way to treat the animals.

She did not set herself in judgment upon the method of handling the horses, for she knew she was utterly ignorant of the conditions. Yet she was sorry for them, and especially pitied the mothers and their young.

The stream of horses was nearly an hour in passing the observation point Rhoda Hammond had selected. The creatures kept on at a swinging canter; never at a walk. Hurrying, snorting, sweating with fear of they knew not what! The odor and dust that rose from the seemingly endless stream of animals finally became rather unpleasant in the nostrils of the onlookers. But they were held there until all should have passed.

By and by the last clattering hoof of the herd was gone, the rear brought up by a bunch of the very young and their mothers, as well as some few lame ones. Then Dan MacCormack, red-bearded and black-eyed, rode by with the rest of the herdsmen, raising his sombrero to Rhoda and her friends.

At the extreme tail of the procession came the chuck wagons of the four outfits, each drawn by four mules with flopping ears and shaved tails, the drivers smoking corncob pipes, and the cooks lolling beside them on the seats, their arms folded.

"Now we'll go," said Rhoda, it being possible to speak in an ordinary tone once again and be heard. "When we get out of the canyon we'll circle around the herd and precede it to Rolling Spring Valley, where the branding pens are set up."

Grace rubbed her gloved hand tenderly over the scar on her pony's hip and said to him:

"Did it hurt you very much when they burned you with the nasty old iron?" He pricked his ears forward and whisked his tail, so Bess said, in a most knowing way, as though he remembered the indignity clearly. "I don't believe I want to see the branding done," she added. "That ugly 'XL' doesn't improve his appearance."

"That is 'Cross L' not 'XL'; and the brand is not so disfiguring as some," Rhoda said. "It helps sell a lot of horses for daddy. His brand is known all over the country."

"That fact doesn't make it any the less cruel," Grace said, with some spirit. "How would you like to be branded, Rhoda Hammond?"

"We-ell," drawled Rhoda, "you know, I'm not a horse."

They clattered out of the canon at last, well behind the train, and then swerved directly west to escape the dust-shrouded herd. Their ponies were still excited, and Rhoda warned her companions to keep them well in hand.

Skulking among the rocks at the edge of the plain, they saw several tawny creatures whose eyes were evidently fixed longingly on the herd of horses.

"Coyotes," said Rhoda. "They haven't a chance, unless a colt goes lame and loses its mother."

"Why don't we shoot them?" demanded Walter eagerly.

"They are not worth the powder we'd waste," declared Rhoda. "And then, they are sort of scavengers. We would not think of shooting a vulture; so why not let the coyotes live—out here? When they sneak around the poultry runs, that's another thing."

Two hours past noon the party rode down a broad green slope into a well-watered valley. A river ran through its length, and several small tributaries joined it. More than one grove of noble cottonwood trees graced the river's banks. The grass was lush, offering pasturage for thousands of cattle, although there was not a horned creature in sight The herd of horses would be contented here as soon as their alarm had passed.

There was a camp by the riverside, and a tent was set up beside the special chuck wagon Mr. Hammond had sent over from Rose Ranch. But Rhoda's father had not arrived at this rendezvous when the little cavalcade rode down to the encampment.

Ah Foon's assistant, a smiling Mexican lad, had prepared lunch, and the girls and Walter certainly were ready for it. It was fully two hours later before the other chuck wagons lumbered info view. (They had passed the herd which would be allowed to drift down into the valley during the evening, guarded by all the hands until daybreak the next day.)

Mr. Hammond appeared, and Rhoda told him at once about the cavalcade of horsemen that she and her friends had seen riding over the saddle of the old Spanish Trail so early in the morning. The ranchman betrayed considerable interest in the matter.

"Did you count 'em?" he asked his daughter.

"There must have been all of a dozen. I could not make out the number exactly," Rhoda said.

"Well," her father grumbled, shaking his shaggy head, "we've got our hands full just now, that's sure. But we don't need to worry about stranglers while there's so many of us down here. And there are plenty of the boys up at the house and with the cows. Reckon it's all right."

"Do you suppose," whispered Nan, "that those Mexicans have come over here for some bad purpose, Rhoda?"

"Maybe they are bandits, like that Lobarto you told us about," said Grace.

"Maybe they will bury treasure somewhere around here," Bess put in eagerly. "And I say, Rhoda: When are we going to get up that party to hunt for Lobarto's treasure?"

"Not until after this round-up, that's sure," laughed the girl of Rose Ranch.

The young people went down to the corrals and branding pens and were told, in the course of time, by Hesitation Kane that the corrals would accommodate a thousand horses at once. It was believed that three days would be occupied in handling the great mob of stock that had been driven down from the hills.

Strange cowboys began to drift into the camp; but all seemed well behaved, and they were the easiest men in the world to get along with. They all put themselves out to give the visitors any information in their power.

"We're going to have a bully time here," Bess declared to Nan. "I do not really want to go to bed to-night. I'd rather hang about the campfires and listen to the boys who are off watch tell stories."

But Rhoda would not agree to this, and the four girls retired at a reasonable hour. Walter slept under one of the cook wagons, rolled up in a blanket like the cowboys themselves. Everything seemed peaceful when they went to bed, and there surely was no sign of one of the tornadoes Mr. Hammond had talked about. The girls, at least, slept just as soundly in their tent as they had in the beds at the ranch house.

The camp was aroused betimes the next morning. Breakfast was eaten by starlight. Immediately the first gang of horses, cut out of the main herd, was driven down.

Walter and the girls were in the saddle as early as anybody. Of course, none of the visitors could swing a rope; but Rhoda showed them how to ride on the flank of the herd and keep the young and wild horses from running free. They had all to be driven into the wide entrance to the corral.

It was inside this barrier that the cowboys rode among the frightened herd and roped those that were to be branded. Even Rhoda did a little of this before the day was over, and her friends thought it was quite wonderful that she showed no fear of the plunging and squealing horses.

But they were much interested, even if the smell of scorching flesh was not pleasant. Walter declared he was going to learn to throw a lariat. But his sister shook her head and shut her eyes tight every time she saw a glowing iron taken from one of the fires.

"Never mind," Nan said. "It is enormously interesting, and we shall likely never see the like again. Just think of growing up like Rhoda, among scenes of this kind. No wonder she seemed different from the rest of us girls when she came to Lakeview Hall."

CHAPTER XVIII

THE OUTLAW

The first day of the round-up was done, and well done, Mr. Hammond said. The girls had been in the saddle for more than twelve hours; and how they did sleep this second night under canvas!

Bess wanted to say something about plans for hunting the Mexican bandit's treasure before she fell asleep; but actually she dropped into slumber in the middle of the word "treas-ure" and never finished what she was going to say.

Nan, however, awoke long before dawn again. She felt lame and stiff, like an old person afflicted with rheumatism. The unusualness of the previous day's activities caused this stiffness of the joints and soreness of her muscles.

She heard the fires crackling and saw the reflection of firelight on the side of the tent, so she knew the cooks were astir. But nobody else seemed to be moving yet, and Nan might have turned over for another nap had it not been for a peculiar sound which suddenly smote upon her ear, and seemingly from a long way off.

After hearing this for a minute or two, she got up and crept to the tent entrance. The flap was laid back for the sake of ventilation, and with her kimono hunched about her shoulders, she crouched in the doorway and looked out across the open space before the grove in which the camp was pitched. It was just between dark and dawn when strange figures seem to move in the dimness of out-of-doors. Yet Nan knew there really was nothing stirring there on the plain. The herd was much farther away.

The sound that had disturbed her came to her ears again, a high, thin, crackling whistle—a most uncanny noise.

"What can it be?" murmured Nan aloud.

"Nan!" whispered a voice beyond her.

"Goodness! Is that you, Walter Mason?" she demanded, huddling her robe closer about her.

"Yes. Come on out. Do you hear that funny noise?"

"Yes. What is it? I can't come out. I'm not dressed."

"Well, get dressed," he said, chuckling. "I want to know what that— There! Hear it again?"

The high whistling sound rose once more. It seemed to be coming nearer, and was from the north, the direction of the hills.

"Isn't it funny?" gasped Nan. "Shall I ask Rhoda?"

"Come on out and we'll ask one of the men if he knows what it is. That horse wrangler is up. I just saw him going toward the pony corral."

"Hesitation Kane? Well, we'll never learn if we ask him," giggled Nan. "Wait, Walter. I'll come right out."

She went softly back to her cot and sat down on it to draw on her stockings. She dressed as quickly and as quietly as possible. Even Rhoda did not awake, and, knowing that all her girl friends were probably just as tired and stiff as she was, Nan got out of the tent without disturbing them in the slightest.

"Oh, Walter!" she murmured, seizing his hand in the dusk, "how strange everything seems. Such a wilderness! And I haven't washed my face."

"Come on down to the brook," said her boy friend. "They call it a river here. They ought to see the Drainage Canal!" and he laughed. "What do you suppose they would say to the Mississippi River?"

"Just what Rhoda said she thought of it when she first saw that noble stream: That it was an awful waste of land to put so much water on it! You know there are sections of this country down here where it rains only once in about eight years."

They reached the river's edge. It was light enough here to see what they were about. Both knelt down and laved their faces and hands and, as Nan said, "wiggled the winkers out of their eyes."

Walter produced a clean towel, for Nan had forgotten hers, and one on one end and one on the other, they dried their faces and hands. Nan's hair was in two firm plaits, and she would not dress it anew until later.

"I don't want to wake up the tribe. They are sleeping so soundly," she explained.

"There's that funny call again!" exclaimed Walter, stopping in a vigorous scrubbing of his face with the towel to listen.

"Come on!" cried Nan under her breath. "We must find out what that means."

They started for the campfire where the cooks were at work, and ran, clinging to each other's hand. Before they reached the cleared space about the Rose Ranch chuck wagon, a figure loomed up before them.

"Here's Mr. Kane now!" cried Nan, halting before the grim-visaged horseman. "Good-morning, Mr. Kane!"

The man's lips twisted into a smile, and he nodded. But no word came from him. Nan was not to be put off easily. She asked:

"Do you know what that sound is, Mr. Kane? Do listen to it!" as the high-pitched whistle again reached their ears.

Hesitation Kane struggled to answer—and it was a struggle. They could see that. He flushed, and paled, and finally blurted out a single word:

"Outlaw!"

With that he strode by and was lost in the shadows of the trees. Nan and Walter gazed at each other in both amazement and amusement.

"What do you know about that?" demanded the boy.

"Well, we got him to say something," sighed the girl.

"But—but it doesn't mean anything. 'Outlaw,' indeed! Does he mean to tell us that there is a Mexican bandit, for instance, out there whistling?"

"How foolish!" laughed Nan. "Of course not."

"Then, Miss Sherwood, please explain," commanded Walter.

"You'd better ask Mr. Hesitation Kane to explain."

"And get another cryptic answer? No, thanks! I want to know—There it is again!"

The sound was closer. Nan suddenly laughed.

"Why," she cried, "I know what it is. It's a horse—a wild horse. Of course!"

"But he said 'outlaw.' Oh!" added Walter suddenly, "I know now. Some of the wild stallions never can be tamed. I've read about them. Of course, it is a stallion. We heard them calling day-before-yesterday."

"Well, I never!" chuckled Walter. "That fellow had me fooled. I didn't know but we were about to be attacked by Mexican robbers."

"Oh, Walter! do you suppose they were desperadoes who came through the Gap day-before-yesterday morning?" Nan asked.

"I don't know. Maybe Rhoda and her father were fooling."

"But they take it so coolly."

"They take everything coolly," said the boy, with admiration. "I never saw such people! Why, these cowboys do the greatest stunts on horseback, and make no bones of it. No circus or Wild West show was ever the equal of it."

"Hullo, here's Rhoda now!"

The Rose Ranch girl appeared, smiling and wide awake. She did not appear to be lame from the previous day's riding.

"Hear that renegade calling out there?" she asked. "He's followed the herd down from the hills. Come on and let's catch our ponies. We'll take a ride out that way before breakfast. If it is the horse I think it is, you'll see something worth while."

They hurried down to the corral where the riding ponies were. With her rope Rhoda noosed first her own, then Nan's, and then Walter's mounts. The saddles hung along the fence, and they cinched them on tight to the round barrels of the ponies, and then mounted.

The horses were fresh again, and started off spiritedly. The sun was coming up now, and again the wonder of sunrise on the plains impressed the girl from Tillbury.

"It is just wonderful, Rhoda," she told her friend. "I shall never cease to marvel at it."

"It is worth getting up in the morning to see," agreed Rhoda, smiling. "There! See yonder?"

The level rays of the sun touched up the edge of the plain toward which they were headed. Here the broken rocks of the foothills joined the lush grass of the valley. On a boulder, outlined clearly against the background of the hill, stood a beautiful creature which, in the early light, seemed taller and far more noble looking than any ordinary horse.

"Oh!" gasped Nan, "is that the outlaw?"

The distant horse stretched his neck gracefully and blew another shrill call. He was headed toward the herd which was now being urged into the valley by the punchers. The horse whistled again and again.

"What a beautiful creature!" murmured Nan. "Oh, Rhoda! can't we catch him?"

"That's the fellow," said the Western girl. "They have been trying to rope him for three seasons. But nobody has ever been able to get near enough to him yet. He is not a native horse, either."

"What do you mean by that?" asked Walter curiously.

"You know, horses ran wild in this country when the Spanish first came in. These were of the mustang breed. The Indian pony—the cayuse—was found up in Utah and Idaho. Horse-breeders down here have bought Morgan sires and other blooded stock to run with the mustangs.

"That fellow yonder was bought by Mr. Duranger, an Englishman, who owned the Long Bow. The horse got away five years ago and ran off with the wild herd, and now he is the wildest of the bunch. And swift!"

"What a beauty!" exclaimed Walter.

The sunlight shone full on the handsome horse. He was black, save for his chest, forefeet, and a star on his forehead. Those spots gleamed as white as silver. His tail swept the ground. His coat shone as though it had just been curried. He stamped his hoofs upon the rock and called again to the herd that he had trailed down from the fastnesses of the hills.

"If we could only catch him!" murmured Nan.

Rhoda laughed. "You want to catch that outlaw; and Bess wants to find the Mexican treasure. I reckon you'll both have your work cut out for you."

CHAPTER XIX

A RAID

The branding of the horses had drawn from ranches all about every man that could be spared. There were upward of a hundred men, including the camp workers and cooks, in the Rolling Spring Valley for those three days.

And how they did work! From early morning until dark the fires in the branding pens flamed. Roped horses and colts were being dragged in different directions all the time. Those already branded, and selected for training on the several ranches, were driven away in small bunches.

The whistling outlaw went away after a day. None of the boys had time to try to ride him down, although there was scarcely a man of the lot who did not covet the beautiful creature.

Rhoda and her friends did about as they pleased while the branding was going on; only they did not ride out of the valley. Nan began to suspect that the reason Rhoda would not lead them far from the riverside encampment could be traced to the appearance of the Mexican riders whom they had glimpsed coming over the old Spanish Trail in the Blue Buttes. Nothing more had been heard of those strangers; but Nan knew Mr. Hammond had warned his men all to keep a sharp lookout for them.

It was when everything was cleared up and the outfits were getting under way for their respective ranches, the last colt having been branded, that a cowboy riding from the south, and therefore from the direction of the Long Bow range, came tearing across the valley toward the encampment by the cottonwood trees.

"Something on that feller's mind besides his hair, I shouldn't wonder," observed Mr. Hammond, drawlingly, as he sat his horse beside the group of girls ready then to turn ranchward. "Hi! Bill Shaddock," he shouted to the Long Bow boss, "ain't that one of your punchers comin' yonder?"

"Yes, it is, Mr. Hammond," said Bill.

"Something's happened, I reckon," observed Mr. Hammond, and he rode down to the river's edge with the others to meet the excited courier.

The river was broad, but shallow. The lathered pony the cowpuncher rode splattered through the stream and staggered on to the low bank on their side. Bill Shaddock, who was a rather grimly speaking man, advised:

"Better get off an' shoot that little brown horse now, Tom. You've nigh about run him to death."

"He ain't dead yet—not by a long shot," pronounced the courier. "Give me a fresh mount, and all you fellows that can ride hike out behind me. You're wanted."

"What for?" asked Mr. Hammond.

"That last bunch of stock you started for our ranch, Bill," said the man, in explanation, "has been run off. Mex. thieves. That's what! Old Man's makin' up a posse now. Says to bring all the riders you can spare. There's more'n a dozen of the yaller thieves."

Further questioning elicited the information that, a day's march from the headquarters of the Long Bow outfit, just at evening, a troop of Mexican horsemen had swooped down upon the band of half-wild horses and their drivers, shot at the latter, and had driven off the stock. Two of the men had been seriously wounded.

"Oh! isn't that awful?" Grace Mason said. "Is it far from here?"

"Is what far from here?" demanded Rhoda.

"Where this battle took place," replied the startled girl. "Let us go back to the house—do!"

But the others were eager to go with the band of cowboys that were at once got together to follow the raiders. Mr. Hammond, however, would not hear to this proposal. He would not even let Walter go with the party.

"You *young* folks start along for the house," he advised. "Can't run the risk of letting you get all shot up by a party of rustlers. What would your folks ever say to me?" and he rode away laughing at the head of the cavalcade chosen to follow the Mexican horse thieves.

"No hope for us," said Walter, rather piqued by Mr. Hammond's refusal. "I would like to see what they do when they overtake that bunch of Mexicans."

"If they overtake them, you mean," said Bess. "Why, the thieves have nearly twenty hours' start."

"But they cannot travel anywhere near as fast as father and those others will," explained Rhoda. "Dear me! it does seem as though the Long Bow boys ought to have looked out for their own horses. I don't like to have daddy ride off on such errands. Sometimes there are accidents."

"I should think there would be!" exclaimed Nan Sherwood. "Why! two men already have been wounded."

"Just like the moving pictures!" said Bess eagerly. "A five-reel thriller."

"You wouldn't talk like that if Mr. Hammond should be hurt," said Grace admonishingly.

"Of course he won't be!" returned Bess. "What nonsense!"

But perhaps Rhoda did not feel so much assurance. At least she warned them all to say nothing about the raid by the Mexicans when they arrived at Rose Ranch.

"Mother will probably not ask where daddy has gone; and what she doesn't know will not alarm her," Rhoda explained.

All the bands of horses for the home corrals had been driven away before the lumbering chuck wagons started from the encampment. Rhoda and her friends soon were out of sight of the slower-moving mule teams.

They did not ride straight for Rose Ranch; but, having come out of the valley, they skirted the hills on the lookout for game. Rhoda and Walter both carried rifles now, and Nan was eager to get a shot at something besides a tin can.

The herd of horses had gone down into the valley, of course; therefore more timid creatures ventured out of the hills on to the plain. It was not an hour after high-noon when Rhoda descried through her glasses a group of grazing animals some distance ahead.

"Goodness! what are they?" demanded Bess, when her attention had been called to them. "Chickens?"

"The idea!"

"They don't look any bigger than chickens," said Bess, with confidence.

"Well," drawled Rhoda, handing her glass to the doubting one, "they've got four legs, and they haven't got feathers. So I don't see how you can make poultry out of them."

"Oh, the cunning little things!" cried Bess, having the glasses focused in a moment on the spot indicated. "They—they are deer!"

"Antelope. Only a small herd," said Rhoda. "Now, if we can only get near enough to them for a shot—"

"Oh, my! have we got to shoot them, Rhoda?" asked Grace. "Are they dangerous—like that puma?"

"Well, no," admitted the Western girl. "But they are good to eat. And you will be glad enough to eat roast antelope after it has hung for a couple of days. Ah Foon will prepare it deliciously."

"Come on, Nan," said Bess, "and take a squint through the glasses. But don't let Grace look. She will want to capture them all and keep them for pets."

But Nan was looking in another direction. Along the western horizon a dull, slate-colored cloud was slowly rising. Nan wondered if it was dust, and if it was caused by the hoofs of cattle or horses. It was a curious looking cloud.

CHAPTER XX

THE ANTELOPE HUNT; AND MORE

The little party approached with caution the spot where the antelopes were feeding. Rhoda was no amateur; and she advised her friends to ride quietly, to make no quick motions, and as far as possible to ride along the edge of the rising ground.

Of course, the wind was blowing from the antelopes; otherwise the party would never have got near them at all. The creatures were feeding so far out on the plain that it would, too, be unwise to try to creep up on them behind the rocks and bushes among which the cavalcade now rode.

"When we get somewhat nearer, we shall have to ride right out into plain sight and run them down," Rhoda said. "That is our best chance."

"The poor little things!" murmured Grace. "They won't have a chance with our ponies."

"Oh, won't they?" laughed Rhoda softly. "I guess you don't know that the antelope is almost the fastest thing that ever crossed these plains. Even the iron horse is no match for the antelope."

"Do you mean to say they can outrun a steam engine?" asked Bess in wonder.

"Surely."

"Then what chance have we to run them down?" demanded Nan.

"Well, there are two ways by which we may get near enough for a shot," Rhoda explained. "I have been out with the boys hunting antelope, and they certainly are the most curious creatures."

"Who are? The cowboys?" asked Bess.

"Yes. Sometimes," laughed Rhoda. "But in this case I mean that the antelopes are curious. I've seen Steve get into a clump of brush and stand on his head, waving his legs in the air. A bunch of antelopes would come right up around the waving legs, and as long as the wind blew toward him instead of toward the antelopes, they would not run. So all he had to do when he got them close enough was to turn end for end, pick up his gun, and shoot one."

"I don't suppose you girls would care to try that," Walter said, his eyes twinkling. "But I might do it."

"Only trouble is," said Rhoda, after the laugh at Walter's suggestion, "I don't see any brush clumps out there. Do you?"

"No-o," said Nan. "The plain is as bare as your palm."

"Exactly," Rhoda agreed. "So we must try running them down."

"But you say they are very speedy," objected

"Oh, yes. But there are ways of running them," said Rhoda. "We will ride on a little further and then let our ponies breathe. I'll show you how you must ride."

Nan was looking back again at the cloud on the horizon. "Isn't that a funny looking thing?" she said to Bess.

"What thing?" asked her chum, staring back also.

"It is a cloud of dust—perhaps?"

"Who ever saw the like!" exclaimed Bess. "Say, Rhoda!"

The Western girl looked around and made a quick gesture for silence. So neither of the Tillbury girls gave the cloud another thought.

They came at length to a piece of high brush which, with a pile of rocks, hid them completely from the herd of peacefully grazing animals. Peering through the barrier, the girls could see the beautiful creatures plainly.

"So pretty!" breathed Grace. "It seems a shame—"

"Now, don't be nonsensical," said Bess practically. "Just think how pretty a chicken is; and yet you do love chicken, Grade."

"Softly," warned Rhoda. "We do not know how far our voices may carry."

Then she gave the party the simple instructions necessary, and they pulled the ponies out from behind the brush and rocks.

"At a gallop!" commanded Rhoda, and at once the party made off across the plain.

Rhoda rode to the west of the little herd of antelopes; Walter and the other girls rode as hard as they could a little to the east of them. Almost at once the antelopes were startled. They stopped grazing, sprang to attention, and for a minute huddled together, seemingly uncertain of their next move.

The four riders encircling them to the north and east naturally disturbed the tranquillity of the deer more than that single figure easily cantering in a westerly direction. Swerving from the larger party, the wild creatures darted away.

And how they could run! The ponies would evidently be no match for them on a straight course. But as the larger number of pursuers pressed eastward, the antelopes began circling, and their course brought them in time much nearer to Rhoda. It was an old trick—making the frightened but fleet animals run in a half-circle. Rhoda was cutting across to get within rifle shot.

The breeze soon carried the scent of the pursuing party to the nostrils of the antelopes, too; but they did not notice Rhoda. She brought up her rifle, shook her pony's reins, and in half a minute stood up in her short stirrups and drew bead on the white spot behind the fore shoulder of one of the running antelopes.

The distance was almost the limit for that caliber of rifle; but the antelope turned a somersault and lay still, while its mates turned off at a tangent and tore away across the plain.

It was several minutes before Walter and the other girls rode up. Rhoda had not dismounted. She was not looking at the dead antelope. Instead, she had unslung her glasses again and was staring through them westward—toward the slate-colored cloud that was climbing steadily toward the zenith.

When the ponies were halted and the sound of their hoofs was stilled, the young people could hear a moaning noise that seemed to be approaching from the direction toward which they were facing at that moment—the west.

"Oh!" cried Nan, "what is that?"

"Have you seen it before?" demanded Rhoda, shutting the glasses and putting them in the case.

"Yes."

"I wish I had," Rhoda said. "Hurry up, Walter, and sling that antelope across your saddle. Look out that the pony doesn't get away from you. Maybe he won't like the smell of blood. Quick!"

"What is the matter?" cried Bess, while Grace began to flush and then pale, as she always did when she was startled.

"It is a storm coming," answered Rhoda shortly.

"But, Rhoda," said Bess, "the wind is blowing the wrong way to bring that cloud toward us."

"You will find that the wind will change in a minute. And it's going to blow some, too."

"Oh, my dear!" exclaimed Nan, under her breath, "is it what your father warned us about?"

"A tornado?" cried Walter, from the ground where he was picking up the dead antelope.

"I never saw a cloud like that that did not bring a big wind," Rhoda told them. "We've got to hurry."

"Can we reach home?" asked Bess.

"Not ahead of that. But we'll find some safe place."

"What's that coming?" cried Nan, standing up in her stirrups to look toward the rolling cloud.

"The wagons," said Rhoda. "See! The boys have got the mules on the gallop. Their only chance is to reach the ranch."

"But can't we reach the house?" demanded Grace, trembling.

"I won't risk it—There! See that?"

The slate-colored cloud seemed to shut out everything behind the flying wagons like a curtain. The breeze about the little cavalcade had died away. But Rhoda's cry called attention to something that sprang up from the site of the mule-drawn chuck wagons, and flew high in the air.

"A balloon!" gasped Bess.

"A balloon your granny!" exclaimed Walter, tying the legs of the antelope to his saddle pommel. "Go ahead, girls. I'll be right after you."

"It was a wagon-top," explained Rhoda, twitching her already nervous pony around. "They did not get it tied down soon enough."

"Then a big wind is coming!" Nan agreed.

"Come on!" shouted Rhoda, setting spurs to her mount.

"Oh, Walter!" shrieked Grace, her own pony following the others, while Walter and his mount remained behind.

But the boy leaped into the saddle. He waved his hand to his sister. They saw his mouth open and knew he shouted a cheery word. But they could not hear a sound for the roaring of the tornado.

In a second, it seemed, the tempest burst about them. Rhoda had headed her pony for the hills. The mounts of the other girls were close beside Rhoda's pony. But Walter was instantly blotted out of sight.

Whether he followed their trail or not the four girls could not be sure.

CHAPTER XXI

IN THE OLD BEAR DEN

"Girls! Oh, girls!" shrieked Grace. "Walter is lost!"

She might have been foolish enough to try to draw in her pony; but Rhoda, riding close beside her, snatched the reins out of Grace's hand.

"More likely he thinks we are lost!" Rhoda exclaimed so that Grace, at least, heard her. Then she shouted to the others: "This way! This way!"

"Wha-at wa-ay?" demanded Bess Harley. "I—I'm going every-which-way, right now!"

But, in a very few minutes, it appeared that this sudden tempest was nothing to make fun over. The four girls, keeping close together, entered suddenly a gulch, the side of which broke the velocity of the wind. They stood there, the four ponies huddled together, in a whirl of dust and flying debris.

"Shout for him!" commanded Rhoda. "Don't cry, Grace. Walter is quite smart enough to look out for himself."

"Don't be a baby, dear," Nan said, leaning forward to pat Grace's arm. "He will be all right. And so shall we."

"But not standing here!" exclaimed Rhoda, after they had almost split their throats, as Bess declared, shrieking for the missing boy. "We must go farther up the gulch. I know a place—"

"There goes my hat!" wailed Bess.

"You'll probably never see it again," said Rhoda. "Come on! Maybe Walter will find us."

"But he doesn't know this country as you do, Rhoda," objected Nan.

"He'll know what to do just the same," Rhoda said practically.

"He will if he remembers what your father told us," said Bess.

"What's that?" demanded her chum.

"Mr. Ham-Hammond said to lie do-own and hang on to the grass-roots," stammered the almost breathless Bess. "And I guess we'd better do that, too."

"Come on. I'll get you out of the wind," said Rhoda, jerking her horse's head around.

The other animals followed. Whether the three Eastern girls were willing to be led away by Rhoda or not, their mounts would instinctively keep together.

Around them the wind still shrieked, coming in gusts now and then that utterly drowned the voices of the girls. Rhoda seemed to have great confidence, but her friends felt that their situation was quite desperate.

The deeper they went into the gulch, however, the more they became sheltered from the wind. This was merely a slash in the hillside; it was not a canyon. Rhoda told them there was no farther exit to the place; it was merely a pocket in the hill.

"It has been used more than once as a corral for horses," she explained. "But there's an old bears' den up here—"

"Oh, mercy!" screamed Grace. "A bear!"

"Hasn't been one seen about here since I was born," declared Rhoda quickly. "But that old den is just the place for us."

Within ten minutes they reached a huge boulder that had broken away from the west side of the gulch. Behind it was an opening among other rocks. Indeed, this whole rift in the hillside was a mass of broken rock. It was hard for the ponies to pick a path between the stones. And it had grown very dark, too.

The other girls would never have dared venture into the dark pocket behind that boulder had Rhoda not led them. She dismounted, and, seizing her pony's bridle, started around the huge rock and into the cavity.

"Must we take in the horses, too?" cried Bess. "I never!"

"I won't balk at a stable, if we can get out of this wind," Nan declared. "Go ahead, Gracie, dear. Don't cry. Walter will be all right."

"But do you think we shall be all right?" asked Bess of her chum, when Grace had started in behind Rhoda.

"I guess we'll have to take Rhoda's word for it," admitted Nan. "This is no place to stop and argue the question, my dear."

She made Bess go before, and she brought up the rear of the procession. It was as dark as pitch in that cavern. The entrance was just about wide enough for the horses to get through, and not much higher than a stable door.

"Here we are!" shouted the Western girl, and by the echoing of her voice Nan knew that Rhoda must be in a much larger cavern than this passage.

The others pressed on. The ponies' hoofs rang upon solid rock. The roaring of the tornado changed to a lower key as they went on. From somewhere light enough entered for Nan to begin to distinguish objects in the cave.

The horses stamped and whinnied to each other. Nan's pinto snuggled his nose into her palm. The animal's satisfaction in having got into this refuge encouraged the girl.

"Well, I guess we're all right in here," she said aloud. "The ponies seem to like it."

"Cheerful Grigg!" scoffed Bess. "My! I never thought I'd live to see the time that I should be glad to take refuge in a bears' den."

"O-o-oh, don't!" begged Grace.

"Don't be a goosie," said Bess. "The bear won't hear us. He must be dead a long time now, if he hasn't been heard of since Rhoda was born."

"Well, you know, bears hibernate," ventured Grace Mason. "They go to sleep and don't wake up, sometimes, for ever and ever so long."

"Not for fifteen years," laughed Rhoda.

Just then, to their surprise, not to say their fright, there came to their ears a most startling sound out of the darkness of the cave!

It was a more uncanny noise than any of the young people had ever in their lives heard before. Rising higher, and higher, shriller and yet more shrill, the sound seemed to shudder through the cavern as though caused by some supernatural source. There was nothing human in a single note of it!

"Oh!" whispered the shaking Grace, "is that a bear?"

"Never in this world!" exclaimed Nan.

"I don't know what it is," asserted Bess. "But if it is a bear, or not, I hope it doesn't do it again."

"Rhoda, what do you think?" demanded Nan, in an awed undertone.

"Hush!" returned the Western girl. "Listen."

"I don't want to listen—not to that thing," declared Bess, with conviction. "It's worse than a banshee. Worse than the black ghost at the Lakeview Hall boathouse."

Once more the noise reached them; and if at first it had startled the four girls, it now did more. For the ponies whose bridles they held, showed disturbance. Grace's mount lifted his head and answered the strange cry with a whinny that startled the echoes of the cavern like bats about their ears.

"Oh, don't, Do Fuss!" commanded Grace. "Don't be such a bad little horse. You make it worse."

"He surely would not have neighed if that was a bear shouting at us," declared Bess.

"Bear, nonsense!" scoffed Rhoda.

"Well, put a better name to it," challenged Bess.

For a third time the eerie cry rang out. The noise completely silenced Rhoda for the moment. Nan said, with more apparent confidence than she really felt:

"One thing, it doesn't seem to come nearer. But it gives me the shakes."

"It can't be that terrible wind blowing into the cavern by some hole, can it?" queried Bess.

"You are more inventive than practical, Bess," said her chum. "That is not the wind, I guarantee."

"But what is it, then?"

"I wish I could tell you, girls. But I really cannot guess," admitted the girl of Rose Ranch, at last.

"You never heard it before?" queried Grace.

"I certainly never did!"

"Say! I ho-ope I'll never hear it again," declared Bess.

But her hope did not come true. Almost immediately the prolonged subterranean murmur echoed and reechoed through the cavern, dying away at last in a choking sound that frightened the quartette of girls deplorably.

Grace began to sob. Nan and Bess were really frightened dumb for the time. Rhoda Hammond felt that she should keep up their courage.

"Don't, Gracie. Don't get all worked up. There must be some sensible explanation of the sound. It is nothing that is going to hurt us—"

"How do you know?" demanded Grace.

"Because, if it was any animal that might attack us, it surely would have come nearer. And it hasn't. Besides, if it were a dangerous beast, the ponies would have shown signs of uneasiness long since."

In fact, this was a very sensible statement, and Nan Sherwood, for one, quite appreciated the fact.

"Of course you are right, Rhoda. We are in no danger."

"You don't know that," grumbled Bess.

"Yes, I do. Unless the sound is made by some human being. And that seems impossible. There is no wild man about, of course, Rhoda?"

"Not that I ever heard of," said the girl of Rose Ranch. "Nobody wilder than our cowboys," and she tried to laugh.

"Well, then, we must not pay any attention to the noise," said Nan, the practical.

"Come on, now," said Rhoda, starting to one side with the pony she led. "Bring them all over here and I will hobble them. Then we can find some place to sit down and wait for the storm to pass. It will rain terribly after the wind. It always does."

"That is all right, Rhoda. I had forgotten about the tornado," said Bess. "What I want to know is: Have you got your rifle safe?"

"Of course. And it is loaded."

"Then I feel better," Bess declared. "For if that dreadful thing—whatever it is—comes near us, you can shoot it."

"I can see plainly," laughed Nan, "that you do not believe the noise is supernatural, Bess."

"Humph! maybe you could shoot a ghost. Who knows?"

CHAPTER XXII

AFTER THE TEMPEST

The party had not got away from the scene of the round-up so very early in the morning; and the detour to reach the herd of antelopes had taken considerable time. It was therefore well past noon when the tornado had sent the four schoolgirls scurrying for the old bears' den.

But by that time it was almost pitch dark outside as well as inside the cavern. The tornado had quenched the sunlight and made it seem more like midnight than mid-afternoon.

The situation of the girls in the cavity in the west side of the gulch might not have been so awe-inspiring had it not been for the mysterious noise that had echoed and reechoed through the hollow rock.

Rhoda hobbled the horses in the dark at one side of the cave, and did it just as skillfully as though she could see. It seemed to the other girls as though fooling around the ponies' heels was a dangerous piece of work; but the ranch girl laughed at them when they mentioned it.

"These ponies don't kick, except each other when they are playing. I wouldn't hobble them at all, only I don't know where they might stray in the dark. There may be holes in here—we don't know. I don't want any of you to separate from the others while we are in here."

"Don't you be afraid of that, Rhoda," said Grace Mason earnestly. "I am clinging to Nan Sherwood's hand, and I wouldn't let go for a farm!"

"As it happens, Gracie," said Bess Harley's voice, "you chance to be hanging to my hand. But it is all right. I am just as good a hanger as you are. I don't love the dark, either."

Nan herself felt that she would not be fearful in this place if it had not been for the queer sound from the depths of the cave. Whatever it was, when it was repeated, and the horses stamped and whinnied as though in answer, Nan felt a fear of the unknown that she could scarcely control.

"What do you think it is, Rhoda?" she whispered in the ranch girl's ear. "It is so mournful and uncanny!"

"It's got me guessing," admitted the ranch girl. "I never heard that there was anything up here in the hills to be afraid of. And I don't believe it is anything that threatens us now. But I admit it gives me the creeps every time I hear it."

On the other hand the roaring of the tornado was heard for more than an hour after they entered the cave. They had come so far from the mouth of the old bears' den that the sound of the elements was muffled.

But by and by they knew that sound was changed. Instead of the roaring of the wind, torrents of rain dashed upon the rocks outside the cave. The girls ventured through the tunnel again, for Rhoda assured them that very heavy rain usually followed the big wind.

"Daddy says the wind goes before to blow a man's roof off, so that the rain that comes after can soak him through and through. Oh, girls!" exclaimed their hostess, who was ahead, "it certainly is raining."

"I—should—say!" gasped Bess.

The moisture blew into the cavern's mouth; but that was not much. What startled them was that they were slopping about in several inches of water, and this water seemed to be rising.

"There's been a cloudburst back in the hills," declared Rhoda. "This gulch runs a stream."

"Oh, poor Walter!" cried Grace, sobbing again. "He'll be drowned."

"Of course not, goosie!" said Bess. "He's on horseback."

"But if this gulley is full of water—"

"It isn't full," said Nan. "If it were running that deep, we'd be drowned in here ourselves."

"We are pretty well bottled up," admitted Rhoda, coming back from the entrance, out of which she had tried to peer. She was wet, too.

"The water is a roaring torrent in the bottom of the gully. You can see it has risen to the mouth of this cave, and is still rising.

"But we need not worry about that. The floor of the cavern inside is even higher than where we stand. It would take an awfully hard and an awfully long rain to fill this cavern. And I don't imagine this will be a second deluge."

Her light laugh cheered them. But it was an experience that none of them was likely to forget. Rhoda's courage was augmented by the actions of the ponies. Those intelligent brutes showed no signs of fear—not even when the mysterious sound was repeated; therefore the ranch girl was quite sure no harm menaced them.

Time and again the girls ventured through the tunnel. The water did not rise much higher; but it did not decrease. Nightfall must be approaching. Bess and Grace both wore wrist watches; but they had no matches and it was too dark to see the faces of the timepieces.

The girls were growing very hungry; but that was no criterion, for they had eaten no lunch. Time is bound to drag by very slowly when people are thrust into such a position as this; it might not be near supper time after all.

"I do hope we shan't have to stay here over night. Can't we wade out through the gully, Rhoda?" Grace asked.

"As near as I could judge, the mouth of this cave was about ten feet higher than the bottom of the gulch," returned the ranch girl. "The water seems still to fill the gulch as high as the entrance. Can you wade through ten feet of water?"

"Oh!" murmured Grace.

"Wish I had a pair of Billy's stilts," said Bess. "It might be done."

"Do you suppose they will come hunting for us?" Nan asked.

"Who?" asked Rhoda practically. "Let me tell you, every boy on the place will be having his hands full right now. I don't think the main line of the tornado struck across toward the house. At least, I hope not. But I bet it has done damage enough.

"If it hit the herds of horses—those wild ones—good-by! They will all have to be rounded up again. And the cattle! Well, make up your minds the boys are going to have their hands full with the herds for a couple of days after this. They won't have time to come hunting for a crowd of scared girls."

"Oh!" said Grace again.

"And why should they?" laughed the ranch girl. "We are all intact—arms and legs and horses in good shape. I guess we will find our way home in time."

"But Walter?" asked Walter's sister.

"He may be home already. Anyway, I don't believe he drifted into this gulch behind us. He missed us somehow."

Just the same she kept going to the mouth of the tunnel to try to look out. And it was for more than merely to discover if the rain had ceased. Secretly she, too, was worried about Walter.

Gradually the rain ceased falling. Nor did the water rise any farther in the tunnel's mouth. But the heavens must still be overcast, for it continued as dark outside the cave as in.

Finally Nan had an idea that was put into immediate practice. She broke the crystal of Bess's watch and by feeling the hands carefully made out that the time was half past six.

"That's half past six at night, not in the morning, I suppose," said Bess lugubriously. "But, oh, my! I am as hungry as though it were day-after-to-morrow's breakfast time."

"Oh, we'll get out of here after a while," said Rhoda cheerfully. "We shall not have to kill and eat the horses—"

"Or each other," sighed Bess. "Isn't that nice!"

Again they ventured out to the mouth of the tunnel. The strange screaming back in the cave had begun again, and all four of the girls secretly wished to get as far away from the sound as possible. The water had fallen, and the rain had entirely ceased. There was only a puddle in a little hollow at the mouth of the cave. The roaring of the stream through the gorge was not so loud.

"It will all soon be over—What's that?"

Nan's cry was echoed by Grace: "Is it Walter? Walter!" she cried.

A figure loomed up from around the corner of the boulder that half masked the entrance to the old bears' den. But the figure made no answer to the challenge. Surely it could not be Grace's brother!

"Who's that?" demanded Nan again.

Meanwhile Rhoda had darted back into the cave. Dark as it was, she found her pony and drew the rifle from its case. With this weapon in her hand she came running to the entrance again, and advanced the muzzle of the rifle toward the figure that had remained silent and motionless before the frightened girls.

CHAPTER XXIII

THE LETTER FROM JUANITA

"You'd better speak up *pronto!*" exclaimed the girl from Rose Ranch in an unshaken tone. "I'm going to fire if you don't."

"Oh, Rhoda!" shrieked Bess.

"It *isn't* Walter!" exclaimed Grace.

"Speak! What do you want? Who are you?" demanded the courageous Rhoda.

"No shoot, Thenorita!" gasped a frightened voice from the looming figure. "I go!"

In a moment he was gone. He had disappeared around the corner of the boulder.

"For mercy's sake!" gasped Bess, "what does that mean?"

"Who was it?" asked Nan again.

"A Mexican. But he wasn't one of our boys," said Rhoda. "I never heard his voice before. Besides, if he had been from the ranch he would not have acted so queerly. I don't like it."

"Do you think he means us harm?" queried Nan.

"I don't know what he means; but I mean him harm if he comes fooling around us again," declared Rhoda. "I never heard of such actions. Why! nine times out of ten he would have been shot first and the matter of who he was decided afterward."

"Why, Rhoda! how awfully wicked that sounds. You surely would not shoot a man!" Bess Harley's tone showed her horror.

"I don't know what I would do if I had to. There was something wrong with that fellow. Let me tell you, people do not creep up on you in the dark as he did—not out here in the open country—unless they mean mischief. If a man approaches a campfire or a cabin, he hails. And that Mexican—"

She did not finish the sentence; but her earnestness served to take Grace's mind off the disappearance of Walter. She had something else to be frightened about!

Rhoda was not trying to frighten her friends, however. That would be both needless and wicked. But she remembered the fact that there were supposedly strangers in the neighborhood, and she did not know who this Mexican lurking about the mouth of the bears' den might be.

The girls went back into the cave and sat down again. Rhoda held the rifle across her lap, and they all listened for sounds from the entrance to the cave. But all they heard was the stamping of the horses and now and then the shrill and eerie cry from the depths of the cavern.

When they made another trip to the mouth of the tunnel, it seemed to be lighter outside, late in the evening as it was, and the torrent in the gulch had receded greatly.

"I believe we can get out now," said Rhoda. "You take the rifle, Grace. You are the best shot. And I will go after our ponies."

"Oh, no! I would be afraid," gasped the girl. "Give the gun to Nan."

So Nan took Rhoda's weapon while the ranch girl went to unhobble the ponies and lead her own to the cave's mouth. The other three followed docilely enough.

Nan did not expect to fire the rifle if the Mexican—or anybody else—should appear. But she thought she could frighten the intruder just as much as Rhoda had.

When the latter and the ponies arrived, Bess uttered a sigh of relief.

"I certainly am glad to get out of that old hole in the ground. It's haunted," she declared. "And I want to get away from this place and keep away from it as long as we are at Rose Ranch. This has been one experience!"

"And you wouldn't have missed it for a farm," Nan said to her. "I know how you'll talk when we get back to Lakeview Hall."

"Oh! won't I?" and Bess really could chuckle. "Won't Laura turn green with envy?"

They mounted their ponies after pulling up the cinches a little, and Rhoda again went ahead. The ponies splashed down into the running stream; but they were sure-footed and did not seem to be much frightened by the river that had so suddenly risen in the bottom of the gulch.

They were only a few minutes in wading out of the gully. When the party came out on the plain the ponies were still hock deep in water. The whole land seemed to have become saturated and overflowed by the cloudburst.

"When we do get a rain here it is usually what the boys call a humdinger," said Rhoda. "Now, let's hurry home."

Just as she spoke there sounded a shout behind them. The girls, startled, drew in their horses. The latter began to whinny, and Rhoda said, with satisfaction:

"I reckon that's Walter now. The ponies know that horse, anyway."

The splash of approaching hoofs was heard after the girls had shouted in unison. Then they recognized the voice of the missing boy:

"Hi! Grace! Nan! Are you there?"

"Oh, Walter!" shrieked his sister, starting her pony in his direction. "Are you hurt?"

"I'm mighty wet," declared Walter, riding up. "Are you all here?"

"Most of us. What hasn't been scared off us," said Bess. "And, of course, we are starved."

"Well, I hung on to the antelope. Want some, raw?" laughed the boy. "Cracky! what a storm this was."

"It was pretty bad," said Nan.

"What happened to you?" asked Rhoda.

"I missed you, somehow. I don't know how it was," said the boy.

"You must have tried to guide your pony," Rhoda said.

"Yes."

"That is where you were wrong. He would probably have found us if you had let him have his head."

"Well, I got under the shelter of a rock out of the wind," the boy said. "But when it began to rain—blooey!"

"Well, thank goodness," said Nan, "it is all over and nobody is hurt."

"But, oh, Walter!" cried his sister, "we got into a haunted cave, and Mexicans came to shoot us, and Rhoda threatened to shoot them, so they went away, and—"

"Whew! what's all this?" he demanded. "You are crazy, Sis."

"Not altogether," laughed Nan. "We did have some adventure, didn't we, girls?"

And when Walter heard the particulars he agreed that the experience must have been exciting. He rode along beside Nan in the rear of the others, as they cantered toward the ranch house, and he put a number of questions to her regarding the mysterious sound in the cavern.

"It must have been the wind," said Nan. "Though it didn't sound like it."

"What did it sound like?" asked her friend.

"I don't know that I can tell you, Walter. It seemed so strange—shrill, and sort of stifled. Why! it was as uncanny as the neigh of that big horse we saw calling to the herd the other morning."

"The outlaw?" asked Walter.

"Yes."

"Maybe it was another horse," he said doubtfully.

"How could that be? In that cave? Why didn't it come nearer, then? Oh, it couldn't have been another horse."

"I don't know," ruminated Walter. "You saw that Mexican, too. There may have been some connection between him and that sound."

"How could that be possible?" asked Nan, in wonder.

"Well, if he had a horse, say? And he had hidden it deeper in the cave? And had hitched it so it could not run away? How does that sound?"

"Awfully ingenious, Walter," admitted Nan, with a laugh. "But, somehow, it is not convincing."

"Oh, all right, my lady. Then we will accept Grace's statement that the cave is haunted," and he laughed likewise.

They arrived at the ranch house within the next two hours. They found everything about headquarters quite intact, for the tornado had swept past this spot without doing any damage. Mrs. Hammond met them in a manner that showed she had not become very anxious, and Rhoda had warned her friends to say little in her mother's hearing about their strange experience.

Nor was anything said to Mrs. Hammond regarding the raid by the Mexican horse thieves. She supposed her husband was absent from the house because of the tornado. That, of course, had scattered the cattle tremendously.

The girls themselves did not think much just then of the stolen horses and the posse that had started on the trail of the thieves. But another incident held their keen interest, and that connected with renegade Mexicans.

There was a letter waiting for Rhoda when she arrived—a letter addressed in a cramped and unfamiliar hand. But when she opened it she called her friends about her with:

"Do see here! What do you suppose this is? It's from that funny girl, Juanita O'Harra."

"From Juanita?" asked Nan. "More about the treasure?"

"Oh! The treasure!" added Bess, in delight. "I had almost forgotten about that."

"Listen!" exclaimed the ranch girl. "She writes better English than she speaks. I should not wonder if there were an English school down in Honoragas."

"Is she home again, then?" demanded Nan.

"So it seems. Listen, I say," and Rhoda began to read:

"'Miss R. HAMMOND,

"'ROSE RANCH.

"'*Dear Miss*:—

"'I have arrived to my mother at Honoragas, and I take this pen in hand to let you know that Juan Sivello, Lobarto's nephew, who has come from the South—he is one of those who lisp—'"

"What does she mean by that?" interrupted Bess, in curiosity.

"The Mexicans of the southern provinces—many of the—do not pronounce the letter 's' clearly. They lisp," explained Rhoda. "Now let me read her letter." Then she pursued:

"'—one of those who lisp—and it is said of him that he has of his uncle's hand a map, or the like, which shows where the treasure lies buried at Rose Ranch. This news comes to my mother's ears by round-about. We do not know for sure. But Juan Sivello is one bad man like his uncle, Lobarto. It is the truth I write with this pen. Juan has collected together, it is said round-about, some men who once rode the ranges with Lobarto, and they go up into your country. For what? It is too easy, Miss. It is—'"

"Oh! Oh!" giggled Bess. "What delicious slang!"

"I guess foreigners learn American slang before they learn the grammar," laughed Rhoda.

"What else, Rhoda?" cried Grace.

"It is to search out the treasure buried so long ago by Lobarto. If the map Juan has is true, he will find it. Then my mother will lose forever what Lobarto stole from our hacienda. Is it not possible that the Senor Hammond, thy father, should get soldiers of the Americano army, and round up those bad Mexicanos and Juan Sivello, take from him the map and find the treasure? My mother will pay much dinero for reward.

"'Believe me, Senorita R. Hammond, your much good friend,

"'JUANITA O'HARRA.'

"She doesn't sound at all as she talked that day she caught me in the woods, Nan," added Rhoda with a laugh.

"The poor girl!" commented Nan. "I wish we could find her mother's money."

"Say! I wish we could find all that treasure for ourselves," cried Bess. "No use giving it all to your Juanita."

"Do you suppose, girls," said Rhoda thoughtfully, "that those men we saw coming through the gap in the Blue Buttes were this Sivello and his gang?"

"Are they horse thieves?" cried Bess.

"Why not?"

"And how about that fellow you were going to shoot over at the bears' den?" asked Grace suddenly. "Why, Rhoda, that fellow lisped. He said 'Theniorita.' I heard him."

The other girls all acclaimed Grace Mason's good memory. Spurred by her words they all recalled now that the strange man who had so frightened them at the mouth of the bears' den had used in his speech "th" for "s."

CHAPTER XXIV

UNCERTAINTIES

The quartette of girl chums from Lakeview Hall and Walter Mason, to whom the girls at once revealed the contents of Juanita's letter, were greatly excited over the Mexican treasure and the seekers therefor.

Without doubt the Mexican girl at Honoragas had written the truth, as she knew it, to Rhoda. Lobarto, the bandit, had met his death five or six years before. It seemed quite probable that he should have sent word to his relatives in the South of the existence of his plunder and the place where he had been forced to cache it. When he was chased out of American territory, the treasure he had left behind would become a legacy for his relatives if they could find it and were as inclined to dishonesty as Lobarto himself.

This nephew of the old bandit chief, Juan Sivello, seemed eager to find the hidden treasure; and if he was really supplied with a diagram indicating the location of the cache, Juan would probably make a serious attempt to uncover it.

The question was, as Walter Mason very sensibly pointed out, having come up to Rose Ranch for this particular purpose, would the Mexicans endanger their plans by making a raid on the horses, and so be chased away without securing the buried riches of Lobarto?

"Doesn't seem reasonable, after all, to me," said Walter, "that the Mexicans your father and the cowboys set out in chase of are the same crowd that Juanita says started up here to find the treasure. There are two gangs of 'em."

"You may be right, Walter," said Rhoda.

"It sounds very reasonable," agreed Nan.

"You are a very smart boy, Walter," said Bess. "I don't see how you do it."

Walter gave the last saucy Miss a grin as he pursued the topic: "That fellow who scared you girls out of your seven wits at the bears' den did not belong to the gang of horse thieves. That's a cinch. They were a hundred miles to the southwest of that place, for sure, and heading back to Mexico."

"Reckon you are right, Walter," again agreed Rhoda.

"Why, if that Mexican we saw—the man who lisped—was looking for the buried treasure, perhaps it is right around that den. Maybe Lobarto hid it in that hole."

"I told you that cave was haunted!" Grace cried.

"They say when the old pirates buried their loot they used to leave a dead pirate to watch it," chuckled Bess.

"Believe me!" said Nan, with emphasis, "if that was a dead bandit we heard shrieking in that cave, he must still be suffering a great deal. But I scorn such superstitions. And I should like to go back there with torches or lanterns and look for the treasure-trove myself."

"Fine!" cried Bess. "I'll go."

"Not while that Mexican is around there," objected Grace.

"Why, he was much more afraid of Rhoda's gun than we were of him," Bess told her.

"I don't know how badly he was scared; but I know very well how much I was frightened. Nothing would lead me back there—not even a certainty of riches—unless we have a big crowd with us."

"I don't know that any harm is to be feared from that fellow," Rhoda said. "But until daddy returns and I talk with him, I won't agree to any search. We want to know what these fellows are after, it is true. But daddy will want a finger in the pie," and she smiled.

So they had to possess their souls with patience while they awaited the return of the ranchman. When Mr. Hammond came back on the following day he confessed that the Mexican thieves had got away and over the Border with the band of horses from the Long Bow outfit.

"That big wind comin' up, and the rain followin', spoiled the trail for us," the ranchman said. "Guess you believe now, children, what I told you about our tornadoes, eh?"

"Including the poor pigs' tails being twisted the wrong way—yes, sir," said Bess with gravity. "Oh, it's all true."

When Mr. Hammond heard of their adventures at the bears' den he became serious at once. But it was not the strange noise they heard that disturbed his serenity. It was regarding the unknown Mexican lurking about the gulch.

"Got to look him up. Maybe nobody but some harmless critter. Can't always tell. But there is one sure thing," added Mr. Hammond slowly. "We crossed the trail of that gang of horse thieves where they broke up into two parties. One party skirted the range, going north. We followed the others because they were driving the stolen critters.

"That's the upshot of it—the rats! If what this Mexican girl friend of yours, Rhoda, says is so, that Sivello and his party made a clean-up of the Long Bow horses, and the bulk of them started back for the Border. Maybe their leader and his personal friends came up this way, thinking to make another search for old Lobarto's plunder.

"I swanny! I wish they'd find the stuff and get away with it. Every once in a while a bunch of them comes up here and makes us trouble; and the excuse is always that old Mex. treasure. My idea, they always have their eyes on our cattle and horses. If they don't find the gold, they pick up a few strays, and it always pays 'em for makin' the trip up here."

"But can't you keep the Mexicans from coming here?" asked Walter.

"If they'd keep their thievin' hands off things, I wouldn't care if they hunted the treasure all the time," said Mr. Hammond. "They'll never find it."

"Oh, Daddy!" exclaimed Rhoda, "we were just thinking of hunting for it ourselves. Can't we? Don't you believe—"

"No law against your huntin' for it all you want to," said her father, laughing. "Go ahead. I didn't say you couldn't hunt for it; I only said I did not think it would be found. Lobarto hid it too well."

"But, Daddy! you don't encourage us," cried Rhoda. "And we are all so interested. We want really to find the money so that Juanita and her mother need not be poor."

"Well, well!" exclaimed the ranchman, "do you want me to go out and bury some money, so you can find it?"

"No. But we want some of the boys to go with us. I want to search that old bears' den, and the gulch there, and all about."

"Go to it, Honey-bird," he said, patting her shoulder. "You shall have Hess and any other two boys you want. That's enough to handle any little tad of Mexicans that may be hanging about up there. I'll speak to Hess. Want to go to-morrow?"

This plan was agreed to. Of course the girls and Walter did not want to rest after their exciting experiences at the round-up and afterward.

"All you young people want to do," Mr. Hammond declared, "is to keep moving!"

Walter made certain preparations for a search of the bears' den. One of the cowpunchers chosen to accompany the party was a good cook. Hesitation Kane took a pack horse with more of a camping outfit than would have been the case had there not been four girls in the party.

"I don't see," drawled Mr. Hammond, "how you girls manage to travel at all without a Saratoga trunk apiece. Got your curlin'-tongs, Rhoda? And be sure and take a lookin' glass and white gloves."

"Now, Daddy! you know you malign me," laughed his daughter. "And as for these other girls, they fuss less than any girls you ever saw from the East."

"I don't know. I'm kind of sorry for that pack horse," chuckled her father, who delighted to plague them.

They might have made the trip to the gulch where the girls had taken refuge from the tornado and returned the next day; but they proposed to trail around the foothills for several days. Indeed, even the cowboys in the party had become interested once more in the buried treasure.

"It strikes us about once in so often," said the cook, as they started away from the corrals, "and some of us git bit regular with this treasure-hunting bug. Long's we know the treasure is somewhere hid and there is a chance of finding it, we are bound to feel that way.

Then we waste the boss's time and wear ourselves out hunting Lobarto's cache. Course, we won't never find it; but it is loads of fun."

"I declare!" cried Rhoda, tossing her head, "you are just as encouraging, Tom Collins, as daddy is. I never heard the like!"

CHAPTER XXV

THE STAMPEDE

The enthusiasm of the girls and Walter Mason did not falter, however, no matter how much the older people scoffed at the idea of the treasure hidden by the Mexican bandit being found near Rose Ranch. They went forth from the ranch house with some little expectation of returning with the plunder.

Hesitation Kane, of course, did not try to discourage them. Even a buried treasure could not excite the horse wrangler, in the least.

"I guess an Apache raid would not ruffle Hesitation's soul," Rhoda observed. "He is quite the calmest person I ever saw."

Since the tornado the cattle of the main herd of Rose Ranch had been broken into small bunches and were feeding in the higher pastures. The swales and rich arroyos, in which the grass had been so lush, had been badly drowned out by the flood. It would be several weeks before the lowlands offered good pasturage again.

The visitors learned that where they had camped at the time of the round-up, the river had risen and washed away every trace of the encampment. Indeed, Rolling Spring Valley had been under water for miles on either flank of the main stream. A bunch of young horses belonging to Rose Ranch, having been confined in a small corral, were drowned at that time.

"There went several thousand dollars," Rhoda explained, when she told her friends of the tragedy. "The losses as well as the gains in the ranching and stock raising business are large. If daddy sells a big herd of cattle, or a fine bunch of horses, he takes in many thousands of dollars, it is true.

"But it is hard to compute the profit or loss on the sale. So many things are likely to happen. Perhaps some disease hits the herd. Thousands of cattle may die in some epidemic. Once wolves came down in the winter, when I was little—I remember it clearly—and killed more than a hundred steers within a mile of the house."

"Oh, dear me, Rhoda! don't tell us about any more wild animals," wailed Grace. "I think the West would be a much nicer place if they had tamed all the wild creatures before man ever moved into it."

"You are not much of a sport, Sis," said her brother, laughing. "It must have been really great around here when the buffaloes and Indians ran wild. You can't remember that, Rhoda, can you?"

"I should hope not!" gasped Rhoda. "Do you think I am as old as Mrs. Cupp?"

"Oh! Oh!" cried Bess. "Poor Cupp!"

"I never saw a buffalo," confessed Rhoda. "And I never heard the war whoop. And an Indian in war paint and other togs would scare me just as much as it would Gracie. But daddy remembers them all. He shot buffaloes for the army, scouted for General Pope, chased a part of Geronimo's band into Mexico, and was a Texas Ranger when the Border Ruffians were really in existence. He can tell you all about those times; only mother doesn't let him."

"There! I suppose she doesn't like to hear about savages and other awful things," Grace said, with satisfaction.

"No-o; it isn't that," Rhoda returned with twinkling eyes. "But mother does not let him talk about those times because it makes daddy out so much older than she is!"

Tom Collins, the cook, was a talkative man, if Hesitation Kane was not. Tom reined his pony into the group of young people and began spinning yarns, some of which perhaps had but a thin warp of truth. He thought it was his privilege to "string along the tenderfoots" a little. One thing he told the girls and Walter, however, interested them immensely.

"You know, I came pretty near roping that black outlaw the day of the tornado. Criminy, if I'd got him!"

"Now, Tom, don't tell us that," commanded Rhoda. "You know there isn't a horse on the ranch that can come anywhere near him in speed."

"That's right," admitted Tom. "But I come on him sudden and unexpected."

"How did it happen?" asked Walter.

"Did you know the boss sent me home ahead of you folks from the rodeo? That's how come I didn't get to ride after those raiders with the other boys. I never do have no luck," said Tom. "If it rained soup I wouldn't have no spoon, and a hole in my hat.

"Well, it was this-a-way: I was riding right along yonder, making for the ranch house, and not thinking of nothing—not a thing! Crossing the mouth of one of them gulches—'twasn't far beyond the one where you gals took refuge from the big wind—all of a sudden my pony threwed up his head and nickered, and out of the slot in the hill come trottin' that big, handsome black critter!

"My soul and body!" exclaimed the cowboy earnestly, "if I'd had my rope handy I could have put the noose right over his head! It certainly did give me a shock."

"Humph!" said Rhoda, "it's always the biggest fishes, daddy says, that get away."

"I guess the Big Boss is right," agreed Tom Collins. "That black feller, he swung around on his hind laigs, and he skedaddled up that gulch. I knowed the place. It's just a pocket, and not very deep; but the sides couldn't be clumb by a goat, let alone a hawse.

"So I turns my pony into that hole and I got my rope ready, and says I to me: 'Tom Collins, you're going to either get an awful fall, or you'll be the proudest man on the old Rose Ranch!'"

"And what happened?" asked Walter.

"Well, I dunno. Either I'd been seeing things, or else that blame black outlaw is bad medicine. He seemed to e-vap-o-rate."

"Now, Tom!" admonished Rhoda.

"Honest to pickles, Miss Rhody! I wouldn't fool you 'bout a serious matter. And this is it."

"You mean you lost the horse?" asked Nan.

"In a blind pocket. Yes, ma'am! Criminy! I couldn't believe it myself. I says to me: 'Tom Collins! your cinches is slipped. That's what is the matter.'

"But you know, Miss Rhody," he added to the ranchman's daughter, "your pa don't allow nothing stronger than spring water on the ranch. I was as sober as a Greaser judge trying his brother-in-law for hawse stealin'. That's what!

"That old black capering Satan went flying up that gulch; and me, I pulled my little roan in after him and got my rope coiled. I says to me: 'You ain't astride nothin' but a little roan goat that only knows cows; but you got the chancet of your life, Tom Collins, to make a killin'. That's right!'

"That is a twisty gulch—I'll show it to you while we're up here prospectin'—and all I could hear was old Blackie's hoofs clattering, and once in a while he'd whistle. He's got a neigh like a steam whistle.

"Well," pursued the cowboy, "all of a sudden the noise stopped. I couldn't hear his hoofs nor his voice. And when I got around the next turn that give me a sight of the complete gulch, clear to the pocket, there wasn't no hawse at all. He'd just gone up in smoke, or something. That's what!"

"What became of the horse?" cried Bess Harley.

"There's some joke in it," Rhoda said doubtfully.

"Honest to pickles!" said the cowpuncher earnestly, "I was scared blue myself. I ain't no more superstitious than the next feller. But that certainly got me.

"I rid back to the mouth of the gulch, lookin' all the way, and never seen a hoof print to show me where he'd lighted out for. He couldn't climb the sides of the gulch. And he didn't hide out on me and let me go back and then dodge out o' the gulch.

"No, sir! There he was one minute, then the next he wasn't there at all. I got back to the mouth of the gulch, and there I seen that old tornado a-comin'. You folks had passed me and 'scaped my attention.

"Me and the roan just squatted down under a bank till the wind was over; then we made tracks for the ranch house ahead of the rain. Get soaked? Well, I should say! But somehow I didn't care to stay around where that blame black Satan disappeared hisself so strange-like. No, sir."

"Tom, I think you have been stringing the long bow," declared Rhoda, shaking her head.

"Honest to pickles!" reiterated the cowboy. "Why—why, I'll show you the very hole in the hill where it happened."

They laughed at that; but the Eastern girls and Walter were inclined to believe that the cowboy had told the truth—as far as he knew it. In some way the outlaw had managed to elude him.

"Goodness!" murmured Walter to Nan, "wouldn't it be great to catch that black horse?"

"He's handsomer than your Prince," agreed Nan.

"He is that. I wonder where he went when Tom lost him?"

The treasure-hunting party did not go directly to the gulch in which the girls had had their adventure at the time of the tornado. A part of what Hesitation Kane had on his pack horse was to be delivered to an outfit herding a bunch of steers back in the hills a long distance.

The girls and Walter had agreed to ride that way, stop over night with Steve's outfit, and then work down to the old bear den from the other direction—that is, from the north.

They entered the foothills through a pleasant, winding valley which, had it not been for the marks of the recent cloudburst, would have been a beautiful trail. But it was considerably torn up by the water that had swept through it, a raging torrent.

They found Steve's outfit with the cattle—nearly a thousand head of them—feeding in two cup-shaped hollows chained by a narrow path. The hills were steep and rocky all around these hollows, and a dozen steers abreast would have choked the path between the two pastures. About half of the cattle were grazing in one hollow, and the other half in the second cup.

The outfit gave the party a noisy welcome. These herders of cattle, working sometimes for weeks at a stretch without getting to the ranch house, and seeing only each other's faces, certainly get lonely.

A newcomer is hailed with joy. And of course the daughter of the Rose Ranch owner and her friends were doubly welcome to this outfit.

The tent was set up for the girls; but, as before, Walter roughed it with the cowpunchers. He was enjoying every minute of his experience on the ranch, whether his timid sister did or not!

A soft, balmy evening dropped down about the camp, which was established in the further cup between the hills. As evening approached the cattle from the outside cup were driven into this inner enclosure. They could be cared for at night much more easily in one herd.

Tom Collins and the outfit's cook outvied each other in making supper. Then there followed two long hours of songs and stories and chaff. The boys badgered each other, but were very polite to the girls.

Walter wanted to ride herd with the first watch, and this was agreed to.

"That is, young fellow, you can ride if you can sing," said Steve, the boss of the outfit, gravely.

"Sing? Well, I don't know. What kind of singing? I'm not famous for my voice," admitted the boy.

"Just so's you can sing something the cows like, it'll be all right," Steve told him. "If anything should happen, you have to sing. It keeps the cows from getting nervous."

"Maybe if I sing it will make them nervous," suggested Walter, not so easily jollied.

"You'd better learn Henery's song, here," said Steve. "Henery has one he *calls* 'My Bonny Lies Over the Ocean' an' he sings it in seven different keys and there's forty stanzas to it. And when a cow hears *that*—"

One of "Henery's" boots sailed through the air just then, and Steve had to dodge it. Henry was not on the first watch.

Walter went out with the first crew. Somebody lent him a slicker, for rain was prophesied. Steve said, drawlingly:

"If it keeps on like this so wet, we might's well be in the middle of the Pacific Ocean. It's rained twice in ten weeks."

Walter's instructions were to keep just in sight of the man riding around the herd ahead of him, to take it easy, and not to do anything to disturb the quiet herd. Some of the cattle were lying down chewing their cud; others were moving slowly while they cropped the grass, all headed west. Riding herd seemed, after an hour or two, to be the dreariest kind of work to the Eastern boy.

Then he noticed that there was a chill in the air and that distant lightning played on the clouds to the north. The cattle all got upon their feet. It did not appear that they were really unquiet; yet there was a certain tension in the air that they must have felt, as well as the herders.

Suddenly there was a near-by flash of lightning followed by a peal of thunder. The camp remained quiet; but the cattle began to snort and paw the earth. Each flash showed Walter that the animals were crowding closer and closer together. They were still heading west.

In the light of another dazzling bolt the boy beheld several horsemen riding down the other side of the cup shaped valley—the west side. They were not of this Rose Ranch outfit. Indeed, in that single glance he realized that they were not dressed like the cowpunchers.

Who could these strangers be? He was about to ride faster and overtake one of the other herders and ask, when the thunder seemed to split the firmament right over the valley. A vivid blue flash lit up the whole arena.

Walter saw one of the group of strange horsemen dash down toward the cattle, flying a slicker high over his head. This horseman made a frightful object charging along the front of the already uneasy steers.

The latter wheeled. With loud bellowings and a thunder of hoofs, the herd started east—started full pelt for the narrow opening between the two hollows.

It was a stampede! Walter had heard of such catastrophes; but he had never dreamed that a charging herd of cattle could make so fearful an appearance. His own horse snorted, jumped about, and started to run away with him; and pull at the bit as Walter did, he could not at once gain control of the terrified little beast.

CHAPTER XXVI

WHO ARE THEY?

The encampment of Steve's outfit, and therefore the tent in which the four girls were sheltered, was on the side of the hill to the south of the narrow path connecting the twin valleys. It seemed as though the chuck wagon and tent, as well as the horse corral, were well out of the path of the charging cattle.

But when Nan Sherwood and her companions, awakened by the louder peal of thunder, gazed out of the tent opening and gained, by aid of the lightning, their initial glimpse of the stampede, it seemed as though a thousand bellowing throats and twice that number of tossing horns threatened the encampment.

"Grab your things and get out this way!" shouted Rhoda, leading the retreat through the rear of the tent.

Fortunately the girls had not taken off more than their outer clothing and their boots. They had no cots during this outing, but used sleeping-bags instead. Seizing such of their possessions as they could find in the dark, they followed Rhoda out at the rear and up the hillside.

From below the pandemonium of sound of the enraged and terrified cattle was all but deafening. At the corral the men who had been off watch were mounting their ponies. The girls heard Steve's stentorian voice shouting to Hesitation Kane:

"Can we swing 'em before they clog that cut into the other hollow, Hess?"

"Nope!" and to the girls' surprise the horse wrangler snapped out the answer. "Shoot the leaders and pile 'em up in the gap. Then swing 'em."

"Oh, I don't want to do that," yelled Steve. "The boss will have a fit. Who started this thing, anyway? That fool boy?"

"Oh! where is Walter?" gasped Grace.

But another cowboy from down below shouted:

"It's a put up job. I saw somebody start 'em. They've been stampeded, Steve."

The next moment the hullabaloo of the cattle themselves made human voices unbearable. A flash of lightning showed the front of the herd as it charged up the slight rise to the mouth of the cut.

Ahead of them, riding like mad and using his coiled rope to urge his pony, came a single rider. Another flash of lightning revealed his identity to the girls.

"Walter! Oh, Walter! He will be killed!" shrieked Grace.

Nan Sherwood leaped a pace in advance as though she would go, afoot as she was, to his rescue. Bess covered her face with her hands. Rhoda shouted in so ear-piercing a tone that the men at the corral heard her:

"Save him! Don't let him go under, boys! Daddy will never forgive you if Walter is hurt."

But before she spoke a single rider had left the encampment like a missile from a gun. It was Hesitation Kane, riding low along his horse's neck, and swinging his big pistol in his left hand. He had taken it upon himself to go against Steve's orders.

A fusillade of shots met the forefront of the stampeded cattle just as it seemed Walter Mason must be overwhelmed. It was in the narrow cut between the two valleys. The leaders went down in a heap, and against the ridge made by their bodies the steers directly behind them crashed with an impact like two colliding trains!

The lightning revealed from moment to moment the awful sight. The cattle behind pressed against those ahead. The bellowing beasts were smothered—were crushed—by the score! It seemed to the girls and to Walter, who now had gained control of his pony and came riding back, as though half that herd of mad beasts must be sacrificed.

But Steve and the other herders saw their chance. They swept down on the flank of the herd. The well trained ponies made a living wall against the cattle. The latter began to mill—that is, turn and travel on the herd's own center.

Of course, many dropped and were trampled. It was a situation that took every ounce of pluck in a man's body to go up against that maddened herd. But Steve and his crew did it.

A rider appeared madly from the west. "Get your guns, boys!" he yelled. "It is a raid! Greasers! I seen 'em start the cattle stampeding!"

"You are bringing us stale news, boy," shouted the outfit's cook. "We're going after them Greasers."

He and Tom Collins were already astride their ponies. Rhoda had got into her boots and now she ran and noosed her pony out of the herd, making the cast by the light of the electric flashes. She saddled, mounted, and was away after the two cooks. Walter joined her, followed quickly by Nan. Bess had to stay behind with Grace, who would never have ventured on such an expedition.

They charged down the swale toward the west. Walter shouted to the others what he had seen at the start of the stampede.

"That is it," cried Rhoda. "Mexicans! When daddy hears about this he will be just about wild."

When the little party had swept to the far end of the hollow there were no signs of the Mexicans who had ridden down into the place to stampede the steers. The rain began to fall; but there was not much of that. It was mostly a tempest of thunder and lightning.

The circling cattle swung west finally and came down the valley at a less dangerous pace. The two cooks, with Rhoda, Nan and Walter, remained to meet and turn their front again. By the time the cattle had circled the valley twice, they were leg-weary and their fears were quenched.

It was a hard night that followed for all. Half the gang had to ride herd until daybreak to make sure that the nervous creatures did not start again. The other men and ponies dragged the dead beasts out of the throat of that gap between the two hollows.

More than a hundred were either dead or had to be shot. The bodies had to be dragged out of the way on the hillsides. Otherwise the steers remaining could not have been got out of the pasture.

Rhoda cried. Every carcass dragged out of the way meant a decided loss for Rose Ranch. And the pity of it!

One puncher was sent to the ranch house to report and ask for a beef wagon to come up. But not more than two carcasses could be used by the whole ranch force at this time of year. The weather was too hot.

By morning the path was cleared. Steve said:

"Get 'em out! Get 'em out as soon as possible. Before night the heavens will be black with buzzards and the hills yellow with coyotes. There will be some singing around this place for a day or two."

They drove the exhausted cattle slowly into the outer pasture, and from there headed them deeper into the hills to a larger valley where the herbage was known to be good.

"I don't know who them Mexicans were. I don't believe it was the same outfit that the boss and the Long Bow crowd chased. They got over the Border, I understand," said Steve.

Walter and the girls talked this mystery over by themselves. It puzzled them vastly.

They had come up here to hunt for the Mexican bandit's treasure; and here they had run into a gang of outlaws just as bad as the old Lobarto gang that had been such a scourge to the country six years before.

"I believe the single Mexican you girls saw at the bears' den belonged to this gang that started the cattle stampeding," Walter declared.

"It must be true," agreed Rhoda.

"Then what shall we do? Don't you think you girls had better go back to the ranch house and postpone treasure hunting until the Mexicans are rounded up?"

"And let them find Lobarto's treasure?" demanded Bess. "Maybe that is what they are after."

"Bess says something sensible, that is sure," Rhoda broke in. "I hate to think of any of those mean Mexicans getting the hidden wealth."

"Just think of poor Juanita and her mother," Nan said, agreeing with her girl friends. "These bad Mexicans will never give back any of the money Lobarto stole."

"Scarcely!" exclaimed Rhoda.

"I suppose Walter is speaking for me," said his sister simply. "I know I am timid. But I will stick if you other girls do."

"Hoorah!" shouted Bess, hugging her. "Why! you are getting to be a regular sport. We've got Tom and Mr. Kane with us, besides Frank, the other cowboy. I am not afraid of the Mexicans—not much, that is—whether they are Juan Sivello and his gang or not."

"Hear! Hear!" agreed Nan. "And having done so much harm in this neighborhood, perhaps they have run away a good many miles to escape pursuit. Let us go and take a look in the bears' den, anyway."

And so it was agreed.

CHAPTER XXVII

THE FUNNEL

It was not until the last of the cattle had disappeared through the gap between the hollows, and the chuck wagon likewise had trundled out of sight, that the girls and their party left the encampment which had been the scene of the night's excitement.

It was not impossible—and even Rhoda mentioned it—that they would none of them ever experience again so strenuous an eight hours as that since the beginning of the stampede.

The disaster was one that would be long remembered by the Rose Ranch cowpunchers, as well as by the ranch owner himself. A more disastrous stampede had seldom been known in that vicinity.

Already the coyotes were appearing—slip-footed and sneaking! They began to gorge on the more distant carcasses of the dead cattle before the chuck wagon was out of sight. And around and around overhead the buzzards circled, dropping at last to the ground and pecking at the stiffened carcasses. Bald-headed these vultures, with scrofulous looking necks and unwinking eyes. There was something vile looking about these carrion-crows.

Having no wagon to bother with, Rhoda and her party could take almost any direction they wished out of the valley. Their tent and camp utensils were borne by the pack horse, so they struck into a narrow bridle path over the hills to the southward.

The three men with the girls and Walter were in rather a gloomy mood when they started off. Even Tom Collins seemed to have lost his spirits. To tell the truth, they were all deeply enough interested in the welfare of the ranch to feel depressed because of the money loss to Mr. Hammond.

Rhoda, however, would not allow her visitors to be overshadowed by this trouble for long. She possessed a good share of her father's cheerfulness and dry humor. She began to tell semi-humorous tales of her own experiences about the ranch and on the ranges, and this started Tom and Frank to swapping tales—some of them altogether too ridiculous to be wholly true.

Only Hesitation Kane remained silent; but that made him no different from usual. He even grinned cheerfully under the sallies of his companions.

About midday the little cavalcade wound around a knob of a hill and arrived at the brink of a sheer bank, below which was a pocket in the hillside. Tom Collins had been guiding them for more than an hour, and now he announced this was the place.

"This here's it," he said with confidence. "I run that black outlaw right up into this here pocket and—there he wasn't!"

"Oh, Tom!" demanded Rhoda, "are you sure this is the spot? A flea couldn't hide down there."

"Honest to pickles! I ain't fooling, Miss Rhody," said the cowpuncher earnestly. "When me and my roan come up this fur and seen we didn't see nothin', I was plumb twisted. Says I to me: 'Here, Tom Collins, is where you got to go an' see a spectacles man 'cause you got optical delusions' And I sure thought I had."

"I'd say nothing could get out of that hole, 'cept by the way it run in, 'ceptin' it had wings," said the other cowpuncher.

"Or get down into it, either," Nan Sherwood observed.

"Oh, yes. We can get down there. We'll make a path and do that little thing," Tom rejoined, getting out of his saddle.

The banks all around the sink and as far as they could see along the gully that led into it, were thirty feet or more high, and quite unbroken. At no place could they see where the edge of the bank had been disturbed.

Tom got a spade from the pack horse, and Frank got a bar. They attacked the edge of the bank where, half way down, there was a little slope to the wall. The gravelly soil yielded rather easily to their digging, and they soon had the beginning of a path, down which the hardy ponies would venture.

Nan Sherwood at Rose Ranch

Hesitation Kane went first, and then the other cowboys. The girls from the East were a bit timid; but every pony that descended made the path more easy. The animals were so well trained that all the riders had to do was to cling on and let their mounts have their own way.

"Now, you see, we're down here," said Tom. "But there ain't a pony in this bunch could climb up to the top, even by this path we made comin' down—no, sir! And yet that outlaw done it—or something."

They started down the gulch, looking for a good place to camp for the noon meal. Hesitation still led the pack horse, her line being hitched to his saddle-ring. They all kept a bright lookout on either hand for some possible path to the top of the bank by which the outlaw horse might have tried to get out of the gulch.

Suddenly Hesitation and his mount and the pack horse disappeared. The silent horse wrangler had taken to one side of a huge boulder while the others had passed on the other side. Had the pack horse not vented a frightened squeal the rest of the party might not have noticed so quickly the absence of the two beasts and Mr. Kane, for the latter did not utter a sound at first.

Walter jumped his horse for the place, and then shouted to the others to come. Behind the boulder was only a narrow path between it and a hole—a hole at least twenty feet across.

The sides of this hole were of loose gravel. The pack horse had made a misstep and had started to slide backwards down the gravel bank. The line snubbed to Kane's saddle was all that saved her from going to the bottom.

The horse wrangler could hold her, but that was about all. Frank arrived almost immediately and took a cast of his rope around the pack saddle. Then the two ponies—his own and Kane's—dragged the pack horse on to firm ground.

"'Nuther slip like that and that old pack mare would been in Kingdom Come," said Tom, peering down the funnel-shaped hole. "I say! you can't see the bottom of this here place."

"No. That out-thrust of rock hides whatever lies at the bottom," Walter agreed, likewise peering down. "Say! couldn't your outlaw horse have tumbled down that place?"

"Criminy! do you reckon so?" asked Tom. "He might! Looks probable, don't it?"

He slid out of his saddle and seized a big chunk of rock—all he could lift. He started this sliding down the gravelly bank. In a minute it had slid to the point where the ledge of rock hid from their view the bottom of this sink. Beyond that it disappeared—and there was no sound of its landing.

"Goodness!" cried Nan, who had ridden up to look, too. "Is that a bottomless pit?"

"Might be, Miss," said Collins. "Anyway, I reckon that's where that ol' black Satan of an outlaw went to. Too bad! He must be deader'n a doornail down there."

The mystery seemed to be explained. But Walter was still thoughtful and curious.

"What's over this way?" he asked, pointing to the hill east of the gulch.

"More gullies," Rhoda said. "And somewhere is the bear den we're going to."

"Is it far?" Walter asked.

"It's in the gulch right next beyond this one," said Tom Collins, with confidence.

Walter evidently had something on his mind, but he said nothing more. Only Nan noticed his brown study. But when she asked him what it was about, he only shook his head.

They stopped for lunch, and then went on down the gulch. They were less than a mile, Tom said, from the open plain, when the head of the cavalcade rounded a turn in the gulch and a figure suddenly leaped up from a shady nook—the figure of a man who had evidently been asleep there and had not heard the cavalcade coming.

Rhoda, who was ahead, reached for the rifle under her knee. Nan was amazed at the action of the girl of Rose Ranch, for the fellow standing before them seemed harmless.

He was a Mexican. He wore an enormous straw sombrero, and there was a good deal of silver cord and bangles upon it. He had a sash wound around his waist, and into this was thrust a pair of silver-mounted pistols. But he did not offer to draw them.

Perhaps he instantly apprehended the fact that the girls were well guarded. The cowpunchers and Hesitation clattered forward. The Mexican swept off his sombrero with much politeness, and bowed before the surprised girls.

"Good-day, Thenoritas," he said in Spanish. "Have I startled you, eh?"

As he stood up again his left hand rested on the butt of one of his pistols. Somehow—he did it so quickly that it was startling to Nan and her friends—Hesitation Kane drew his own pistol and thrust it forward.

"Put 'em up!" he commanded.

The Mexican seemed to understand just what the horse wrangler meant. He slowly, and with a deep scowl marring his face, raised his empty hands above his head.

CHAPTER XXVIII

A PRISONER

"It was just like one of those Western photoplays that sometimes come to the Freeling movie palace, and which Mrs. Cupp, the ogress of Lake-view Hall, does not approve of, and never will let us girls attend if she can help it," sighed Bess ecstatically, later on.

Bess Harley was especially fond of such dramas. And Walter, too, took delight in the imaginative if rather crude pictures of the West as it used to be.

But here was the real thing. Even Nan was held breathless by the tense drama. Rhoda's hints and tales of adventure had not altogether prepared her visitors for anything like this.

Hess Kane must have thought that the situation called for the sudden and stern action he had taken. Of course, Nan Sherwood thought, that snaky-looking Mexican was not wearing those two silver-mounted pistols in his sash just for ornament.

Tom Collins slid out of his saddle at a slight gesture from Kane and went behind the Mexican to disarm him.

"Keep your hands up," he said to the fellow. "Our wrangler ain't gifted much with speech, but he's sure a good shot. Where's the rest of your gang?"

"No understand," said the fellow sullenly.

"Mean to say you are alone?" Tom demanded.

"Si, Senor."

"Where's your horse?"

"I am afoot, Senor."

"Stop it! Don't try any of your Mex. jokes. You afoot, and with them spurs on your shanks?" and the cowboy pointed to the enormous silver spurs on the man's boots.

"That's one of the fellows that stampeded them steers last night," said Frank, with conviction.

The Mexican looked startled. His black eyes shot glances around the group which faced him.

"Look out that we're not ambushed," said Rhoda in a low voice. "There may be others around."

"We'll keep our eyes open," said Tom easily. "Guess I'll tie this fellow's wrists, just the same."

He removed his neckerchief as he spoke. He twisted it into a string, and suddenly snatched the Mexican's hands behind him. The fellow exploded some objection in his own language, and would have fought Tom, but Kane thrust the weapon he held forward again and the prisoner subsided.

Meanwhile Bess excitedly whispered to the other girls:

"Do you know who I believe he is? I feel sure of it!"

"Who?" Nan and Grace chorused.

"That Juan Sivello that Mexican girl wrote to Rhoda about."

"I had thought of that," said Rhoda, nodding. "It may be."

"And if it is," whispered Bess, thrilling at the thought, "he's got the diagram of the hiding place where his uncle put all that treasure."

"Goodness me!" sighed Grace, "how rich we should all be if we found it."

"It surely would be great," her brother said.

"And that poor Juanita and her mother would get their money back," Nan added.

"Risk our Nan for remembering the poor and needy," laughed Bess.

"There are others to think of besides that Mexican girl and her mother," said Rhoda seriously. "According to the tales we have heard about Lobarto's treasure, at least half a dozen families had been robbed by him along the Border. And churches, too.

"Some of the haciendas he burned and destroyed the people in them. They could claim nothing, of course. And he had a lot of other plunder that nobody knew who its actual owners were, so the story goes."

"Poor people!" sighed Nan.

"Say! give us a chance to divide a few millions among us," said the reckless Bess. "Who ever heard of treasure-seekers who were not made rich beyond the dreams of avarice when they found the hoard?"

She had spoken rather loudly. The Mexican glanced up at them suddenly and his eyes flashed. He muttered something under his little, stringy, black mustache.

"Look out, Bess," warned Nan. "He heard you then."

"Well, what of it?" demanded the reckless one. "Aren't the boys going to search him' and find that map Lobarto made?"

"My! but you are a high-handed young lady," chuckled Walter.

"What we going to do with him, now we've got him?" asked Tom Collins suddenly.

"Daddy ought to see him, don't you think?" said Rhoda confidently.

"Yep," agreed Hess Kane, returning his pistol to its holster.

"Well, now, I reckon that would be the proper caper," said Tom Collins. "Say, *hombre*," he added, nudging the Mexican, "where's your horse?"

"I am afoot, I tell you," was the reply.

"I can see you are—now," admitted the puncher. "But you'll have a fine walk in those boots to Rose Ranch."

"I will not walk to the Ranchio Rose!"

"Then you'll be dragged," Tom said coolly. "I reckon my little roan can do it."

"No," said Kane. "Put him on the pack mare."

They were all eager to get the young Mexican to Mr. Hammond and see what the shrewd old ranchman could make out of him. The saddle and goods were removed from the pack animal, and cached. For the girls did not intend to give up their treasure-hunting trip— by no means! It was only postponed.

"I'd give a good deal to know what became of the rest of this Greaser's gang," said Frank, the other cowpuncher.

"After they stampeded them steers, maybe they run away," Tom observed.

They put the prisoner astride the saddleless horse and made their way slowly to the ranch house. It was almost bedtime when they arrived, and the family was much surprised to see them at that hour.

"Well, I swanny!" ejaculated Mr. Hammond, "is this the best you girls could pick up-a Greaser? Do you call him a treasure?"

The prisoner's eyes flashed again as he heard this. He stood by sourly enough while the girls explained more fully to the ranchman.

"All right! All right!" growled Mr. Hammond. "If he is one of those that stampeded the steers, he'll see the inside of the jail. I'd like to catch 'em all."

The visitors made their way to bed as soon as they had eaten their late supper; but Rhoda remained with her father when he questioned the Mexican.

At first the prisoner refused to give any information about himself or his business near Rose Ranch. But being an old hand at that game, Mr. Hammond finally made him see that it would be wiser for him to reply. If he did not wish to get others into trouble, he would better try to save himself.

And it soon appeared that the young Mexican did not feel altogether kindly toward the men who had come over the Border with him — whoever they were. There had been some quarrel, and the others had abandoned him, taking even his horse with them when they did so.

"Were you with them when they ran off the Long Bow stock?" asked Mr. Hammond.

"That was not done by us. We separated from those thieves of horse-stealers when they would put their necks in jeopardy," the Mexican said in his own tongue, which both Mr. Hammond and Rhoda understood.

"So you kept out of that, heh? Then you rode up this way?"

"Into the hills," said the other sullenly. "The country is free."

"Not to such as you unless you can give a mighty good reason for being over there. You and your friends have cost me more'n a hundred steers."

"Not me!" ejaculated the prisoner, shaking his head.

"No?"

"I tell you they abandoned me. I do not know where they go."

"And what were you hanging about that place over there in the hills for?" demanded Mr. Hammond. "Come, now! Didn't you give your friends the slip because you wanted to hunt for that old hidden treasure?"

"Senor!"

"Never mind denying it," said the ranchman sternly. "And I reckon I can make another guess. You are Lobarto's nephew. Your name is Juan Sivello. I bet there's a warrant out for you in the sheriff's office at Osaka right now, my boy."

The young Mexican jumped up, startled. Mr. Hammond reached out a hand and pushed him back into his seat.

"Sit down, boy. You'd better make a clean breast of it. I want to know all you know about that old bandit's hoard, or you'll go to the sheriffs office with me in the morning. Take your choice."

CHAPTER XXIX

A TAMED OUTLAW

Rhoda had a great deal to tell her girl friends the next morning. She came into their room before even Nan was up, and curled down on one of the beds to relate to an enormously interested trio all the particulars of her father's interrogation of the Mexican prisoner.

"And is he that Juan What-you-may-call-him?" asked Bess. "Truly-ruly?"

"He is. Daddy made him admit it. And more."

"Go on, dear," said Nan. "You know we are just as curious as we can be."

"Well, I tell you, girls, it was no easy matter to get the truth out of that fellow. But he is scared. He fears being handed over to the American sheriff. He knows that the men he brought up here have got into trouble. They quarreled about the treasure's hiding place. Some of the men had ridden with Lobarto himself, and they thought they knew more about the treasure than this Juan does."

"But the map?" cried Grace.

"Yes. He's got it. But it isn't much of a map. Because daddy knows the country so well, he says he recognizes the places marked on the diagram."

"Oh, bully!" exclaimed Bess Harley.

"Don't be so quick," advised Rhoda. "It is not very clear at the best."

"Oh! Oh!" groaned the too exuberant Bess.

"There are certain places marked on the diagram. Daddy says the cross Lobarto made where the location of the hidden treasure is supposed to be, is on a bare hill. It is the hill between that gulch where we took refuge from the storm that day, and the gully up which Tom Collins says he chased that black horse."

"On the hill, then? Not in a hole at all?" asked Nan.

"That is what makes daddy doubtful. He says to have dug a hole out in the open, on the side or the top of that hill, would have been ridiculous. So he says he doesn't believe in it any more than he did before."

"But can't we go to look?" pleaded Grace.

"Of course we can," agreed Rhoda.

"Let's, then," Bess said, eagerly.

"That's what we will do, Bessie. Daddy says we can have the boys again and a pack horse, and can grub around all we like. Meanwhile he is going to hold on to the Mex. to see what turns up."

"And the others? What of them?" asked Nan.

"Why, we know that a part of his gang went back into Mexico with the stolen horses. Daddy has a posse of our own boys hunting the hills for those scoundrels that scared Steve's steers the other night. He says—daddy does—that he believes those Mexicans started that stampede just to get the outfit away from there. Evidently the gang believed the treasure is buried up that way. They haven't got the diagram, you see."

"That young Mexican must have been looking for the treasure when he came to the mouth of the bear den that time and scared us so," said Nan thoughtfully.

"Yes," Rhoda agreed. "He says he has been scouring the locality."

"And no luck?"

"So he says. But he believes his uncle's map is all right, when once he can understand it."

"I declare!" Nan observed, "I don't see why we can't find the treasure, then, if it is somewhere about the hill."

"We'll dig all over it," said Bess eagerly. "Come on, girls! Let's go today," and she hopped out of bed.

Walter was eager for the second treasure-hunting trip, as well. The party got away before mid-forenoon and took their dinner at the mouth of the gulch in which the bear den was located.

"I tell you what," Walter said to Nan privately, while they were eating. "That cross on the old bandit's map is between this gulch and that other where Tom lost the outlaw."

"Yes. So they say, Walter," Nan replied.

"Do you know, Nan, I've an idea there is a hole right through this hill?" said the boy.

"A hole? You mean that the cavern goes clear through?"

"Clear through to that funnel-shaped place where our pack horse fell down."

"Walter! That's an idea!" admitted Nan.

"Guess it is," he returned, smiling. "Let's get them to search the cavern first. We've got lanterns and a big electric torch. There is one thing I want to assure myself about, too," he added.

"The treasure, of course."

"Something more. I want to know what made that noise that frightened you girls so."

"Oh, Walter! I had forgotten about that. Why remind me?" cried Nan.

"Well, don't remind the others, then," laughed Walter.

Rhoda was quite willing to go to the bear den first of all, and the other girls seemed to have forgotten the noise that had so disturbed them when they took shelter there from the tornado.

This time they left the ponies outside, with Frank to watch them. Tom and Hess Kane entered the cave with the party of young people.

The place was utterly dark and utterly silent. But they soon lit the lanterns, and Walter went in advance with the electric torch.

The main cavern in which the girls had waited for the storm to blow over was of considerable size, as they had thought at that time; and the domed roof was very high. The hill really was a great hollow.

There were passages into several smaller caves; but these were mere pockets beside the larger apartment. Wherever there was any appearance of the floor of the cavern having been disturbed, the men used the spade and bar. But they found no hidden treasure. In fact, the floor was mostly of solid rock. The old bandit would have found it difficult to have buried anything under such flooring.

It seemed as though they had searched the place thoroughly, and all the little chambers, too, when Walter's torch revealed to him a crack in the wall at the far end of the cavity, and almost as high as his head. He soon called the others to come and examine this place.

"A big boulder has been rolled into an opening. That is what it is," said Nan.

"Just what I was saying to myself," Walter confessed. "And I believe nature did not roll the rock here, either."

"Think somebody shut the door on a passage, do you?" asked Tom Collins, curiously. "Bring along the bar, Hess, and let's see."

"If nature did not wedge that rock into the opening, then whoever did it did an excellent job!" growled Walter, after working on the boulder for a couple of hours.

"It's started. Yes, it's started," said Tom complainingly. "But you can't say much more about it and speak the truth. If that old Mexican's treasure ain't behind that rock, then it ought to be, that's sure!"

Supper time came, and they were still working at the boulder. It was agreed to camp in the cavern for the night, and continue working at the wedged rock until bedtime.

"And might as well bring the ponies in and hobble 'em, eh?" suggested Tom Collins. "No use standing watch on 'em outside. They've grazed themselves full this afternoon."

It was so agreed. Hess went out and helped Frank bring in the animals and wood for the cooking fire.

But here was a surprise. Almost as soon as the horses clattered in on the hard floor of the cavern one of them whinnied. Seemingly in response, the reechoing sound that had previously so startled the girls rang faintly through the cavern. But from much farther away, it seemed, than before.

"The haunt!" gasped Bess. "There it is again."

The men and Walter looked inquiringly at each other. Tom Collins shook his head: "Can it be the echo of that little roan of mine squealing?"

"Never!" cried Rhoda. "That doesn't sound like any horse I ever heard. Why, it's queer!"

"Queer's the word; but horse queer," muttered Tom.

Walter looked eagerly at Nan in the lamplight.

"Do you believe that black horse is somewhere here?" she whispered.

"I most certainly do, Nan," he said with confidence.

They worked all the evening on that stone. Occasionally the faint and mysterious sound floated to them. The men would not give their opinion about this, but they were warmly expressive of what they thought about the boulder that had to be moved.

They rolled up in their blankets and sleeping bags finally, and left the rest of the job until morning. Without proper tools to attack the boulder it was a slow and back-breaking task.

In the morning, however, while Tom Collins was getting breakfast and Frank drove the ponies out to graze, Walter and Hess tackled the boulder again. It seemed that at night, when they left the work, they had been just on the verge of prying it loose.

Suddenly it heaved over. It was rounded on the front, so once having turned it, it was an easy matter to get it out of the way. The lantern light showed that there was a passage behind the fallen barrier.

The girls came running at the crash and at Walter's cry. The boy had grabbed up the torch and pressed the switch. He shot the round ray of the lamp into the dark passage.

"Oh! There is no treasure there!" murmured Bess, in disappointment.

Walter ventured in, the others crowding after him. The passage was long and crooked. They traveled at least a hundred yards, the roof of the tunnel being nowhere more than ten feet in height.

Suddenly there was a sound in front. Something scrambled over the rocks. Walter shut off the lamp and they saw daylight ahead of them.

"See here! Here he is!" shouted the boy, hurrying on. "What did I tell you?"

There was more scrambling of hoofs, and then a shrill squeal—surely the noise made by a horse! Hess and the girls following, Walter came to the circular place to which the tunnel led. They all saw what Walter saw. For once Hesitation Kane was surprised into expressing himself suddenly:

"It's the black outlaw or I'm a dodo!"

CHAPTER XXX

TREASURE-TROVE

Hesitation Kane was not a dodo, for nobody could deny that the trembling and snorting creature standing on the other side of this open hole was the beautiful wild stallion that had followed the range horses down from the hills more than a week before.

But such a pitiful looking creature as he was now! The girls expressed their pity for him without stint. Not that he was marred, or seriously injured in any way. But he was so weak from hunger that he could scarcely stand.

It was plain that a few shrubs and some bunch grass had grown in the bottom of this hole. He had eaten them down to the very roots, and then dug the roots up with his hoofs and chewed them.

Tom Collins' story of how he had chased the stallion and the creature had so suddenly disappeared, was now explained. The horse had slipped into the hole in the gulch above, just as the pack horse had. Only the wild horse had slid clear to the bottom of the funnel-shaped hole.

The outcropping ledge hid this opening which was at the level of the caves. Nobody could see the imprisoned horse from above. That, the searching party well knew.

"And to think that he might have starved to death here," murmured Grace.

"Can you get him and tame him, Mr. Kane?" asked Bess Harley.

"But he should be Walter's horse," put in Nan Sherwood, earnestly. "Walter has felt all the time that he was here and that it was he that made the noise that scared us so."

"Of course this is the source of that cry we heard," Rhoda admitted. "When we led the ponies into the big cave that day, he heard them, and they knew he was here. I believe I haven't much sense, girls, after all. I should have known it was another horse squealing."

"I was sure of it last night," said Walter, "when he squealed after Frank drove in the stock."

"Well, daddy is fair," Rhoda declared. "When he learns all about it he will decide who is to have the horse. Of course, he was originally the property of the Long Bow Ranch and that brand is on him now. But daddy will fix it right."

"Say!" suddenly cried Bess, "did this party start out from Rose Ranch to hunt wild horses? I—should—say—not! We are after treasure—"

"Oh, girls, see here!" interrupted Grace Mason suddenly. "What do you suppose this can be?"

While the horse wrangler went for a rope to use in holding and leading the wild horse, Grace had gone back a way into the tunnel. Here the floor of the cavity was not of rock. It was plain to be seen by the light of the lantern that the horse had stood in here and stamped and dug the dirt up with his sharp hoofs.

In a hole that he had thus excavated Grace had seen an object that glistened in the lamplight. "See here," she repeated. "What do you suppose this can be?"

Walter was too busy watching the horse to attend to her. But the other girls came. Nan dropped down on her knees beside the smaller girl. Almost immediately she cried out:

"It is! Oh! Look!"

"Good," said Bess, crowding closer. "I don't know what it is, but I am looking. Mercy me, Nan Sherwood! what is that?"

"A silver candlestick," said Nan in a hushed tone. "Girls, we have found the Mexican treasure!"

Breakfast was entirely forgotten after that. The coffee boiled over back in the big cave, and when Tom thought of it, there was only a little extract of Mocha in the bottom of the burned-black pot!

They brought the spades into play again. They unearthed a cavity in the floor of the passage into which had been heaped haphazard a mass of silver and gold ornaments, vases, bags of jewelry, church plate, and of money in quantity to make them all go half mad with delight. Such a treasure-trove none of them had really believed existed.

They were hours in becoming calm enough to decide what should be done. Then Frank was sent off on the swiftest pony to the ranch house to report to Rhoda's father, and to bring back a wagon in which to carry away the heavier ornaments and vessels that Lobarto had stolen from the churches in his own country. How the bandit had ever brought such a weight of treasure so far was a mystery.

"And there's another thing," Bess Harley said, later. "Why did he make that cross on the map which he sent to his relations, pointing to a cache on the hillside?"

"He didn't," Rhoda rejoined quickly. "He made the mark all right. He meant to show that it was under the hill."

"Of course!" agreed Nan.

The Mexican treasure was bound to make Mr. Hammond a lot of bother, as he said. For when news went abroad that it was found, dozens of people came to Rose Ranch trying to prove that some of it belonged to them.

Many of these claimants were impostors, and the ranchman referred them to the courts which, under the circumstances, could do very little toward straightening out the tangle of ownership.

In the first place, the cavern where the wealth was found chanced to be on land to which Mr. Hammond held the title. Mr. Hammond tried to return the church treasure and vestments; but two of the churches Lobarto had wrecked had never been rebuilt, and the priests were scattered.

The same way with the coined money. The robber had gathered such coin as he had stolen and put it in sacks. Unless a claimant could prove how much money, and just what form of money, was stolen from him, Mr. Hammond saw no reason for handing out the recovered treasure.

Juanita O'Harra and her mother were treated as generously as it was possible. And they were satisfied with Mr. Hammond's judgment. In fact, most of those who really had lost property were too thankful to have a generous amount returned to quarrel about the ranchman's decision.

Mr. Hammond claimed that the party searching and finding the cache had certain rights. The girls, Walter, and the three employees of the ranch on the spot when the find was made, all shared in the treasure-trove.

There was one person who had been hungry for the treasure who did not get a dollar of it. That was the young Mexican, Juan Sivello, Lobarto's nephew. As Mr. Hammond said, chuckling:

"All that chap took away from Rose Ranch was a flea in his ear!"

The letters that went back East after the finding of the Mexican treasure—both to the home folks and to girl chums—were so long and so exciting that one might have doubted if the four girls from Lakeview Hall were quite sane. The visitors to Rose Ranch enjoyed many adventures before they started East again, and they had at the end much more to tell their friends. But nothing so exciting as the result of the treasure hunt.

Walter Mason, too, had an additional prize. Mr. Hammond did not think that the recovered black horse was a fit mount for a boy; but he shipped to Chicago two ponies, for Walter's and his sister's use, in exchange for any rights the boy might think he had in the outlaw.

Nan and Bess had no means of keeping horses at home if they owned them; so when they left Rose Ranch they bade their pretty steeds good-by—perhaps with a few secret tears. For the little beasts had carried them for many miles, and safely, over the ranges.

Life at Rose Ranch never lacked variety, it seemed. Never again would the Eastern girls pity Rhoda Hammond because of her home life, and wonder if she did not miss much that they considered necessary to their happiness and comfort.

"I guess everything has its compensations," said Nan, using a rather long word for her. "I thought my uncle and aunt and cousins up in the Michigan woods must be awfully lonely, and all that. But I found it wasn't so."

"And down here nobody has a minute to spare. You can't even feel lazy yourself," agreed Bess. "I feel right on edge all the time, expecting something new and wonderful to happen."

"And doesn't it?" asked Nan, laughing.

"I should say it did! Why, I never realized so much could happen in a month as happens on Rose Ranch in a single day," agreed her enthusiastic chum. "I wish I had been brought up on a ranch like Rhoda."

"Oh," said Nan Sherwood, "I don't wish that. There is only one place in which to be born and brought up. That's in the little cottage in amity, and with Momsey and Papa Sherwood."

THE END

Copyright © 2023 Esprios Digital Publishing. All Rights Reserved.

Milton Keynes UK
Ingram Content Group UK Ltd.
UKHW050442280324
440101UK00016B/1203